Penguin Cri...
Breath of Su...
Editor: Julia...

D1633248

Elizabeth Ferrars was born in Rangoon and arrived in England at the age of three. She was educated at Bedales School, Hampshire, and took a diploma in Journalism at London University, but decided to write novels instead. She has had about thirty crime novels published on both sides of the Atlantic, and many have been translated into Japanese, German and French.

Elizabeth Ferrars

Breath of Suspicion

Penguin Books

Penguin Books Ltd, Harmondsworth,
Middlesex, England
Penguin Books Inc., 7110 Ambassador Road,
Baltimore, Maryland 21207, U.S.A.
Penguin Books Australia Ltd, Ringwood,
Victoria, Australia
Penguin Books Canada Ltd,
41 Steelcase Road West, Markham, Ontario, Canada

First published in the U.S.A. by
Doubleday 1972
First published by Collins' Crime Club
Published in Penguin Books 1974
Copyright © Elizabeth Ferrars, 1972

Made and printed in Great Britain by
Hunt Barnard Printing Ltd, Aylesbury, Bucks
Set in Intertype Times

Chapter One

To begin with, Richard Hedon had not wanted to go to the Ottershaws' party. He had gone only because Anne Damerel had wanted it so badly. He distrusted this kind of reunion after so many years. Far too many years, he had thought. It was fifteen since Richard, Jerome Ottershaw and Anne Tenbury, as she had been then, had been students together at University College, and if Jerome had really wanted to see Richard during that time, he had known the name of the bookshop, Joseph Hedon and Sons, in Farcet Street, where Richard had worked all that time. The telephone number was in the book. Jerome had needed only to ring up.

In the old days Richard and Jerome had been reasonably close friends. But when Jerome, a biochemist, had gone as an assistant lecturer to Bristol University, they had drifted apart. Both of them also, in the old days, had been a little in love with Anne and she with each of them. She had not yet met Peter Damerel and had been capable of being fecklessly in love with any reasonably attractive man whom she happened to be with. A quality in her that could not have altered more. Once Peter had come into her life, and even after he had gone out of it, finally and for ever, into a hospital from which he had never emerged, Anne had never shown more than a casual interest in any other man. She lived with her two children and her mother in a small house in Barnet, and kept the family, with the help of her own and her mother's pensions, by doing a part-time job for a literary agency. In her work she mixed constantly with men, and at thirty-seven was as good-looking as she had ever been, and surely, Richard thought, might have married again. Yet he knew that he was the only man with whom she went out more than very occasionally, and almost the only one who was ever asked to the house in Barnet. Mainly, he believed, this was because he had known Peter very well. But also Anne had a tendency to cling with tenacious loyalty to anything that went back to the old days, and it was because of this loyalty, Richard was sure, that she had thrown herself with such uncharacteristic enthusiasm into her renewed friendship with Jerome Ottershaw.

She had recently met him by chance, with his wife Jeannie, and had been determined, ever since it happened, to draw Richard back with her into the magic circle of the past. So in the end, to please her, he had agreed to go to the party that the Ottershaws were giving, had picked Anne up at her office, taken her to dinner in Dean Street, then gone on with her to the Ottershaws' flat in Westminster.

They found Jerome standing just inside the door of a large sitting-room, welcoming his guests. Jerome had changed a great deal since Richard had seen him last. Richard himself had not changed much. At thirty-seven he would have been immediately recognizable to anyone who had known him at twenty-two. He was the kind of man whose appearance alters very little between boyhood and middle age, except that, at twelve he had looked exceptionally mature, and now, with forty not far off, looked boyish. He was of medium height, was thin and stooped a little, as he always had, with a look of being in something of a hurry to reach, head down, some unspecified goal ahead of him. A look that was quite misleading. Richard generally took his time to arrive at any important decision, and even after he thought that he had achieved this, was given to second thoughts and third thoughts. He had curly brown hair that flopped forward over his forehead, and a thin face that had developed lines early because of its mobility. He did not look exactly untidy or neglected, yet he generally wore whatever came to hand and once it was on forgot about it. It had been almost by chance, involving some spilled soup on his cord trousers, that he arrived at the Ottershaws' party in his one and only dark suit.

Face to face with Jerome, Richard was glad that that was how things had happened. Jerome had an excellent tailor. He needed one, for he had become distinctly plump with the passage of time. Once he had been lean, pale and intense. Now he was rosy, bland and very well-covered. He was a tall man and his good clothes gave him an air of dignity and success. He was, after his fashion, very successful. He was a Deputy Scientific Adviser in the Council of Productivity and Science, which meant that he was not quite at the top in his world, but near it, and he was wealthy too. His wife Jeannie was the only daughter of a soft-drinks manufacturer in the Midlands, so their standard of living was not limited by Jerome's Civil Service salary.

Jeannie was at the other end of the room when Anne and Richard were shown into it by the Spanish maid, but Jerome's bellow, as soon as he saw Richard, brought Jeannie burrowing her way through her guests towards them. She was a small, fine-boned woman, perhaps ten years younger than Jerome, yet already with grey hair, which she wore with distinction, drawn sleekly off her bird-like face and piled high on her head in an elaborate explosion of curls. She wore long swinging jade earrings, a flame-coloured trouser suit and golden sandals.

Jerome let go of Richard's shoulder, which he had been kneading heavily, to put an arm round Jeannie.

'Here he is, darling,' Jerome boomed in her ear. 'Anne finally got him here. She says she was afraid, right up to the last moment, that he'd duck out. Richard, how in hell have we managed not to run into each other all these years? London's such a village, you'd think we'd have had to come across each other some time. You haven't been avoiding me, have you?'

'Now is that likely?' Jeannie said. For such a small, brittle-looking woman, her voice was unexpectedly rich and deep. It should have gone with a big bosom and voluptuous curves. 'He's simply forgotten about you, that's all. People do forget, you know. I expect the only faces he can really attach the right names to are the ones that belong to those queer customers who actually buy books from him.'

Jeannie was almost right. In recent times Richard had been settling more and more contentedly into the narrow world of the old bookshop, which he owned in partnership with his brother, and had increasingly tended to ignore what went on outside it, while his feeling for those curious characters who came to prowl about in the shop, some of them staying for an hour and leaving with a couple of paperbacks, and others appearing swiftly, like gods, out of nowhere, staying ten minutes and spending five hundred pounds, had become not far off affection.

'Oh, books, books,' Jerome Ottershaw said. 'You always had your future mapped out, didn't you, Richard? You always knew exactly where you were going.'

'And so did you, darling,' Jeannie said. 'Up and up, gathering all sorts of interesting things on the way, one of them being your rich and loving wife.'

'Is being a DSA in the CPS so very high up?' Jerome asked. 'Is it the sort of thing you expected of me in the old days, Richard? A man who hasn't seen the inside of a lab of his own for ten years. Would you ever have prophesied that?'

'Now that you ask me, I suppose not,' Richard said.

'I was dedicated in those days, you know,' Jerome said. 'Blooming well dedicated. Or committed — that's the word everyone likes nowadays, isn't it? What a laugh. Old Jerome Ottershaw committed. It's enough to make you split your sides. And the real joke about it all is that it took a whole five years to dawn on me that all the dedication in the world can't make up for being no bloody good at your job. Ha ha!'

He did not sound in the least bitter about it, but on the whole rather pleased with himself.

Jeannie laughed too and said, 'Darling, the real joke is that you're still dedicated, and to a job at which you happen to be very good indeed.'

'Administration,' Jerome said. 'Don't you know that in the intellectually exalted sphere in which I mingle that's almost a dirty word? Being good at it doesn't excuse one's existence when one's got to stand between some damned fool who wants to grow beans at the bottom of the sea, as I literally had to the other day, and the limitless flow of the country's money. You work for yourself, don't you, Richard, and almost by yourself? God, what I wouldn't give for a life like that! . . . Oh, Jacqueline, Adrian . . . ' He turned from Richard to greet some more new arrivals. 'How lovely to see you . . . Richard, we must have a good talk later. And lunch one day soon . . . Jacqueline, that dress is a miracle . . . '

Richard, a glass in his hand by now, found himself propelled on into the roomful of strangers.

Anne, the only person in it whom he knew, was yards away, talking to a man who looked bewildered, dignified and foreign. Probably she was trying out one of her languages on him. She could speak several, for she and Peter had travelled a good deal. He had been in the Foreign Service and Anne had never been content to batter her way through life with nothing but English.

Richard stood by himself, hemmed in by elbows, with the noise, which seemed to have risen noticeably in pitch even during the time that he had been in the room, making him want to flee. Loud noises gave him a feeling of physical discomfort and utterly confused him. He sipped his drink. It had come out of a large jug and was pale green, with lumps of fruit and cucumber floating about in it, and felt suspiciously less innocuous than it looked or tasted. A girl on a sofa in a far corner of the room who had gone for *vin rosé* had shown her good sense, he thought. She was an arresting-looking girl. She had golden-brown hair and almost amber-coloured eyes, and was apparently ignoring everything around her. Her stillness, her silence in the din were like a beckoning hand to Richard. He began to make his way towards her.

But it was some time before he found himself sitting beside her. His move in her direction was impeded several times by people whom the fruit and cucumber and whatever these were afloat in had made extremely friendly and expansive, and who all seemed to be eager to describe to him the journeys on which they were just about to set out, or from which they had just returned, journeys to Japan, to Jamaica, to East Africa, always at the expense of some government department, or UNESCO, or other public body. It all sounded very glamorous and costly. By the time that he reached the sofa and subsided on to it he felt ashamed to mention the fact that he himself had not been considering anything more ambitious than a fortnight on the West coast of Scotland.

The woman on the sofa was slender and long-legged, and was wearing a plain, long-sleeved, cream-coloured dress with a gold chain belt.

Neither she nor Richard spoke immediately, though they exchanged tentative smiles. It was as if they already felt that they shared something, if perhaps only the sofa. It was an early-Victorian sofa, though with springing modern enough, under the red damask covering, to make it comfortable.

After a moment she said, 'You came with Anne Damerel.'

'Yes,' he said. 'You know her, do you?'

'A little.' She hesitated and with her gaze on his face becoming suddenly strangely piercing, added, 'My name's Hazel Clyro.'

It was as if she were watching to see if the name meant anything to him.

Very faintly it set a bell jangling in Richard's mind. Was she some minor celebrity, he wondered, avidly eager for some sign that he had heard of her? Unluckily he had no idea what had set the bell ringing.

'Clyro is an unusual name,' he remarked.

'He was a most usual man,' she answered.

Richard noticed the past tense, as he had already noticed the wedding-ring on her finger.

She went on, 'You haven't told me who you are.'

'My name's Richard Hedon.'

'Are you a scientist?'

'No. I sell books.'

'It's just that most of the people in this room are scientists. Scientists, or near-scientists, and their wives and mistresses. Friends of Jerome's. Are you a friend of Jerome's?'

'I used to be a good while ago. We were students together.'

'When you were young. That's funny, d'you know, I can't imagine Jerome young. What was he like?'

'Well – he was a lot thinner.'

She laughed. 'So he didn't start life with a middle-aged spread. Not that that doesn't surprise me to some extent. I'm sure he was a very chubby baby.'

'And he was a biochemist.'

'What were you?'

'I did English Literature.'

'Then how did your tracks cross?'

'I think it was in something called the Critical Society.'

'That sounds very imposing. What did you criticize?'

'Do you know, I can't really remember,' Richard said. 'Religion, of course, and war, and art in its various forms, and the laws on homosexuality and abortion, as they were then, and things like that.'

'No politics?'

'I don't seem to remember.'

'Politics don't interest you?'

'Oh, I cast my vote when I get the opportunity.'

'In those days you'd have been too young to have a vote to cast.'

'Yes, that's true.' He looked at her lounging form, relaxed and remote. 'Don't tell me you're one of the people who think it's practically indecent if one isn't passionately interested in politics?'

'Oh, anything but!' Her voice sharpened oddly. 'I want people to see one another just as people, and not always be on one side of some fence or the other.'

'Isn't that what we're supposed to be able to do in our good old democracy?' he said.

'Oh, you mean Conservative and Socialist leaders lunching together at the Athenaeum.'

'And their lowly followers meeting for a pint in the local pub.'

'And their wives joining to get up jumble sales to collect money for refugees from one sort of oppression or another.'

'And people just putting up with one another somehow. Why not?'

She laughed. 'You don't know how burningly I agree with you. Only, you see, my husband . . . Oh, he isn't here,' she added, as Richard started to look round the room. 'He hasn't been around for a long time. Paul Clyro.' Again her gaze fastened intently on Richard's face, as if she were watching for some reaction to the name.

He was beginning to feel more positively that at some time it had meant something to him. And if only Paul Clyro had been, say, some early nineteenth-century writer of no account, who had been forgotten by nearly everybody, Richard would probably have been able to recall immediately the names of every one of his obscure works, and to quote what price, in

11

good condition, they would fetch on the present-day market. But since he was merely a contemporary, Richard's memory of him had faded.

'Is he . . . ?' he began, then faltered.

'Dead?' she said flatly. 'How should I know? There must be people alive who do, but why should you expect that of a mere wife? Tell me some more about this Critical Society. Was Jerome a very outstanding member of it?'

'He was Chairman, as a matter of fact.'

'Which is just right, isn't it? You know, he often talks as if he really suffers because he can't get back to work in a laboratory. He portrays all the agonies of frustration. But I believe people generally end up doing what they were meant to do from the first, and I'm sure Jerome got more kick even in those days out of being Chairman of your Society than out of his biochemistry.'

Richard thought that this might well be true. Yet at the time nothing of the kind had ever crossed his mind. Jerome was four years older than he was. He had been a post-graduate student when Richard had been in his first year. The age gap had seemed enormous, and the interest in him taken by the mature-sceming, enthusiastic young man that Jerome had then been, had been an exciting, stimulating compliment. Richard had been only too ready to take Jerome at his own valuation.

'But you mustn't take any notice of me when I talk about him like that,' Hazel Clyro went on. 'I've always found it difficult to take him completely seriously. But he's a good man, you know, a very kind one. He and Jeannie were both immensely kind to me – when I needed it badly. And so they have been ever since. I'm afraid they find me unrewarding material to work on. I simply can't be their sort of person. But still, I'm grateful. Most truly grateful. If they hadn't helped me, I'm not sure what I mightn't have done.'

'Did your husband leave you?' Richard asked.

'That's a way of putting it.'

'What other ways of putting it are there?'

But before Hazel Clyro could answer, Jerome loomed above them out of the crowd and deposited himself on the arm of the sofa beside Hazel.

He put a hand into her hair and ruffled it gently. There was something affectionately protective in the gesture, as if he were giving reassurance to a nervous child.

'So you've met Richard,' he said. 'I wonder how you'll suit each other. What happens when two awkwardly solitary characters meet? Do you recognize a kindred spirit and enjoy it, or can't you bear the sight of one another?'

'We've been surviving it quite well so far,' Hazel Clyro said. 'We've been talking about you, Jerome. About what you were like when you were young.'

'I'd like to join in,' he said. 'There's nothing like a good old bout of nostalgia. But there's Jeannie signalling frantically. I've got to go and do something about the drinks. She enjoys these affairs, you know. She's one of the very few people I know who honestly do. They're such quaint tribal rituals, aren't they?'

He went away across the room to his wife.

Other people interrupted Hazel and Richard after that, but from time to time during the evening they found themselves together again and she went on asking him questions about Jerome and also about Anne. The relationship that had existed between the three of them when they were young seemed to intrigue her. She talked very little about herself. She worked as a secretary in a big firm of heating engineers, and seemed neither to like nor dislike the job, which to Richard sounded extremely dull. It gave her enough to live on, she said, and that seemed to be all that mattered to her. Richard could discover no obvious enthusiasm in her, but only a glancing, ironic interest in the people round her.

She spoke occasionally of her husband, but the moment that she had done so, she spoke hurriedly of something else. It was almost like a game, a deliberate teasing of Richard. By now he felt sure that the name Paul Clyro was familiar, though he still could not think when he had heard it. Later, Richard thought, he would ask Anne about him. He supposed that she would know.

Thinking of Anne, it occurred to him that it was time to ask her if she wanted to go home yet. The crowd in the room was beginning to thin. As it did so, he began to be aware of the room itself. The furniture in it was early Victorian, the pictures were explosively abstract, the floor was covered from wall to wall in deep olive-green carpet. It was pleasant in its way, yet all looked somehow very recently arranged, like a room in an exhibition, and not as if the Ottershaws had committed themselves to living with it for long. It was very hot, although all the windows were open to the summer night.

Anne's inky dark head was nowhere to be seen. Worried, because he knew that she had been expecting him to drive her home, he asked Jeannie Ottershaw if Anne had left already.

'Oh, ages ago,' Jeannie answered in her vibrant voice. 'She said we weren't to disturb you, some people from Potter's Bar were going to give her a lift. But you aren't thinking of leaving yet, are you? This is the time in a party I always like best, when almost everyone's gone and you can sit down and take your shoes off and pull everyone to pieces. Have some more of this concoction of ours. Nice, don't you think? It creeps up on you so gently. Or would you prefer some whisky? I'm going to shift over to whisky myself.'

So Richard had some whisky and presently, when Hazel said that she must telephone for a taxi, he suggested that he should drive her home.

She lived in a shabby-looking little street in Kentish Town. She yawned a good deal on the drive and said that she did not know why she had stayed on so late, she usually left parties as early as she decently could. Neither she nor Richard talked much. Both seemed to feel that they had talked enough during the evening to have earned the right to a comfortable silence with one another. At the door of her ground-floor flat he got out of the car and helped her out of it, waiting beside her on her doorstep as she felt inside her bag for her key.

Suddenly she went rigid, staring over his shoulder.

'Look! No, don't look – no!' she whispered. 'You'll think I'm mad. Perhaps I *am* mad. Only I'm not, I'm not!'

Sagging against the yellow-painted door of the drab little brick-built house, she shut her eyes tightly, blotting out some vision that had made them blaze wildly in the light of the street lamps. The key in her hand stayed arrested several inches from the keyhole.

Richard, very startled, looked where she was staring. He saw nothing but a grey Cortina going slowly along the street, with the man in the car, who had a high, bald forehead, on which the beam from the street lamp briefly bestowed a gleaming polish, apparently peering at the numbers of the houses. He evidently did not find the one that he wanted, for the Cortina, passing Richard's car, reached the end of the short street, turned to the left and disappeared.

'All the same, you saw him, didn't you?' Hazel Clyro opened her eyes and looked searchingly at Richard. 'The car, that man in it, he was there. You saw him. You saw him looking at us.'

Richard began to feel very uncomfortable. This was not the sort of thing that he had expected when he had offered to drive Hazel home from the party.

He said hesitantly, 'I saw a car . . .'

'A grey Cortina.'

'Yes.'

'With a bald man in it.'

'Yes.'

'Oh God!' Her voice went up half an octave. 'I'm not mad and I'm not drunk, but I'm being driven mad. Is that what they want, d'you think? Aren't they ever going to leave me alone?'

Richard knew that she was not drunk. Sitting beside her for most of the evening, he had seen her sip her way slowly through two glasses of *vin rosé*. But mad? He felt a slight pricking in his scalp. That was another matter. One on which he felt unable to form an opinion. He had encountered people who had been as charming as this woman had been all the evening, as intelligent, as surprisingly delightful to talk to, who had turned out to be far over the brink of sanity. Books, of course, attracted both the sanest and the most insane of mankind, so he had had considerable experience.

Hazel gave a dry little laugh. She had been watching his face.

'Oh well, it doesn't matter,' she said. 'I'm used to him turning up at all sorts of odd times. Sometimes I wonder if I mightn't miss him if he didn't. I'm sorry I said anything about him. Please don't look so worried.'

She unlocked the door, pushed it open and reached inside for the light switch.

The light was in a rather dusty-looking white plastic shade and shone on cream-coloured wallpaper that bore the scars of other people's pictures and a floor of scarred linoleum tiles. It did not seem at all the right background for her.

She said, 'I was thinking of asking you in for a drink, but I don't suppose you want to risk it with someone who believes she's being followed around London by bald men in cars. So good night. And thank you for bringing me home. It was kind.'

She stepped quickly inside.

To the closing door Richard said rapidly, 'Am I going to see you again?'

The door continued to close, then opened again, but only a little way.

'I shouldn't have thought you'd want to, after that little scene.'

'I do want to,' he said.

'But whether I was right about that car, or whether I was talking nonsense, I can hardly be a desirable person to know, can I?'

'That seems beside the point.'

'I'm afraid you're sorry for me.' The door had opened no farther. The big yellow-brown eyes were looking at him through the narrow gap. 'Though of course, the truth may be that you know a lot more about me than you've said. When you say you want to see me, perhaps it's only because you think I'll end up telling you all those things so many people want to know.'

'I don't know anything about you that you haven't told me yourself this evening,' he said.

'Is that really so?' There was a sudden extraordinary hopefulness in her voice, as if nothing could be as wonderful or as improbable as his ignorance of her.

'It's really so,' Richard said.

'Then if you want to see me . . . No, listen, my number's in the book, so there's nothing to stop you telephoning if you want to, is there? But before you do that, will you do something? Ask your friend Anne Damerel about me. She can tell you the whole story. And then perhaps you won't want to telephone after all. It's happened before. Good night.'

She smiled, or rather, made a tight-lipped little grimace that drew the creamy skin of her face into harsh lines. It made her look far more than the thirty-one or two that he had guessed she was. In a way it made her look ageless, as pain or fear can.

The door closed.

Chapter Two

Richard crossed the pavement to his own car. Weaving his way through the emptying streets towards St John's Wood, where he lived with his brother and sister-in-law, he tried to work out what it could possibly mean if that man in the car had really been following Hazel Clyro.

Could he have been police? Could she be involved in something illegal, or at least with people who were? Alternatively, could the man have been a private detective, set to watch her perhaps by her husband, whom she had never said was dead, or by some woman, who was collecting evidence against her own husband? And even if one of those reasons was the right one and the pursuit was not simply a shadow on the girl's mind, was it any reason for Richard to allow himself to be scared off seeing her again? He had never made a habit of allowing other people to interfere much where his feelings were concerned, so why should he let it happen now?

The house in St John's Wood was all in darkness when he reached it. Bernard and Harriet would have gone to bed long ago. The house, a spacious one, built about the turn of the century, was the one in which Bernard and Richard had grown up and it had been left to Bernard by their father. But it was far too large for him and Harriet, who were childless, so they had made a self-contained flat of the top floor and rented it for a very modest sum to Richard.

The arrangement worked very well. They all liked one another, were good at leaving one another alone, yet were companionable too, with an affection that went deep. Richard had long ago slipped into the way of having most of his meals downstairs with the other two, enjoying Harriet's cooking a great deal

2

more than his own, while Harriet liked having someone besides just a husband to care for. There had been a time when she and Bernard had discussed adopting a couple of children, but the appropriate moment for it had somehow gone by, and Richard had inherited a good deal of her unused maternal tenderness. Though warm, this was on the whole unobtrusive, except that she had made up her mind that he ought to marry Anne Damerel, and kept doing what she could to bring this about.

At breakfast on the morning after the Ottershaws' party Harriet wanted to know if he had driven Anne home to Barnet. Had he stayed there with her for some time? Was that why he had been so late? Harriet knew that he must have been later than usual, because she would have heard him come in if she had still been awake at the time.

Richard said that Anne had left early with some other friends and that he had driven another woman home.

Disappointed at first, Harriet soon wanted to be told all that she could get out of him about the other woman.

Richard told Harriet her name, but then came up against a feeling that he could not possibly describe Hazel Clyro. It was not that he had not observed her, but rather that he had observed too much, and when it came to putting it into words, he did not know where to begin.

Harriet said, 'Clyro – why do I seem to know that name?'

She was a short, broad-beamed, muscular woman, uncomplicated in her emotions and abounding in energy. She was nearly fifty, which was five years older than Bernard. She had short, curly, light brown hair, which was turning grey, and direct, thoughtful grey eyes. At breakfast, which they had in the kitchen, she was wearing an old blue dressing-gown and bedroom slippers.

From behind his newspaper Bernard answered, 'Disappeared.'

'What's disappeared?' she asked.

'Clyro,' he said. 'Paul Clyro. Vanished. About two years ago.'

Bernard hardly ever forgot anything. If he had sat there and really thought about it, Richard knew, he could probably have come up with the very date on which this had happened to Paul Clyro.

Bernard, in appearance, was very like Richard, except that he was a little taller, a little heavier, a little slower in his movements. He was altogether a more deliberate man, slower at forming opinions, harder to persuade to change them once they had been formed. He was not argumentative, but simply detached himself from any discussion that was not going the way he wanted.

'That's right,' Harriet said. 'I remember. He was a spy.'

'Not that anyone's ever proved,' Bernard said. 'Not that anyone suspected. It was all very mystifying. He was here today and gone tomorrow, no one ever found out why. That's how it was, according to the papers, anyway. He may have gone behind the Curtain, for reasons best known to himself, or he may simply have fallen off a cliff and been drowned. I didn't know he left a wife. I suppose it's his wife you're talking about. Poor woman.'

'You can bet it's his wife,' Harriet said as she cleared away the dishes that had held cornflakes and brought bacon and eggs to the table. 'Have you ever known Richard take up with a woman who wasn't hopelessly involved with some other man? She *is* still involved with him, I suppose. She's still pining for him. She wouldn't dream of thinking seriously about anyone else. She sounds exactly your type, Richard.'

'I haven't taken up with her,' Richard said. In the light of morning he was hazy about the events of the evening before. The atmosphere of fantasy in which it had ended made everything else about it seem unreal. 'I drove her home, that's all.'

'Clyro was a molecular biologist,' Bernard went on. 'He was the man who found the body of Wolsingham, the man who swallowed a lot of potassium cyanide in his lab just before the security people caught up with him.'

'Oh, Wolsingham – of course!' Harriet said. 'He really was a spy, wasn't he? He'd been handing on scientific stuff to the Russians about germ warfare or something for years.'

'About viruses. That's how it looked. But there was never any trial, of course, because of his suicide. And Clyro was his assistant. Came into the lab late one night and found Wolsingham dead. But there was never any whisper of suspicion against Clyro, at least in public. Then about a year later he vanished.

Went out one day, took no clothes with him, no money, and never came back.' Bernard looked over the top of his paper at Richard. 'What's she like?'

'Quite pleasant,' Richard said. 'She l'ves in Kentish Town. She's a secretary to somebody or other.'

'How informative,' Harriet said. 'Bernard means is she young, is she beautiful, is she interesting, is she tragic?'

After a slight hesitation Richard admitted, 'A bit of all four. And I understand now why she spat out the word politics as if it were a slug dished up in her salad.'

'And she's living for the day when her husband reappears,' Harriet said. 'Richard, I do wish you could see, that sort of woman is so *bad* for you. She'll only bolster up your dreadful tendency not to commit yourself.'

'Perhaps if Clyro came back,' Bernard said, 'he wouldn't be all that welcome, after the way he treated her.'

'Wouldn't he, Richard? Is that so?' Harriet sounded momentarily hopeful. 'No, I don't believe it. That husband will turn out to be an insuperable difficulty, when it comes to the point, just like poor Peter Damerel. The trouble is, you're so stupid. Anyone can see that Anne would marry you tomorrow if she weren't convinced you can't possibly want to take on a widow with two children. And you've got this idea she'll never love anybody but Peter. The way the two of you can't sort out your problems!'

'There are no problems.' Richard got suddenly to his feet. Usually he took Harriet's nagging about Anne good-humouredly, but this morning for some reason he could not stand it. 'Anne and I understand each other perfectly.'

'Famous last words,' Harriet observed as Richard left the kitchen.

He and Bernard did not drive to the shop together that morning, as they often did, for Bernard was attending a book sale at a mansion in Hertfordshire, where a collection of some importance was being sold. The morning had a faint summery mistiness, that promised heat later. Farcet Street was near the British Museum. The shop had two small, neat windows on either side of a rather low doorway, which opened into the ground-floor department which was the unimportant part of the shop, containing a few shelves of glossy-looking modern books and paperbacks, besides some stacks of the commoner second-hand editions. Above there were two more floors, reached by steep, narrow stairs, to which the knowledgeable customer penetrated straight away. Bernard had his office on the first floor, and Richard on the second. The whole place had a faint leathery smell, and although it was well-lit, something about all those brown bindings with the dull glimmer of the gilt lettering on them gave the whole place an atmosphere of shadows. The sounds of the busy street outside hardly penetrated into it.

Richard spent most of the morning dictating correspondence to his secretary, Miss Saxthorpe, a small, brown, leathery woman with a mouse-like quiet about her swift deft movements. She could come and go without his even knowing that she had been in the room. He wasted a good deal of her time that morning by staring, empty-minded, into space. She was very patient with him, only occasionally recalling him, in her little cheep of a voice, to the work in hand. His mind kept wandering to the hazy vision, which was all that he had been able to retain, of Hazel Clyro. The haziness worried him. Why was he not able to see her and to think about her more clearly? Her presence was distractingly there in the room with him, as if she had followed him there and meant to stay with him. He felt haunted by her. Yet he was unable to remember her features clearly.

At a quarter to twelve he was interrupted by one of the girls who worked in the ground-floor department, who came upstairs to tell him that there was a gentleman below who wanted to see him.

'A Mr Ottershaw,' she said. 'He says if it's not convenient not to bother, he'll call in some other time.'

Richard went downstairs. He found Jerome Ottershaw leafing through a volume of Hiller's *Flora of the Eastern Mediterranean*. He was wearing a very well-cut blue suit with a pink shirt and a dark red tie, and looked pink and plumply buoyant and blandly friendly.

'Lovely prints, beautiful reproduction,' he remarked in greeting as he regretfully put the book back on its shelf. 'I wonder who can afford books like that. Well, I was passing, so I called in to see if you've got time for lunch with me. Just an idea. Probably you're up to the eyes.'

Richard wondered how someone with offices in St James's had happened by chance to pass a shop in Farcet Street.

'Nothing I'd like better,' he said.

'Good,' Jerome said. 'How do you like the Europa in Charlotte Street? Do you remember it in the old days? The nice family who used to run it – check tablecloths, splendid food, low prices. The nice family have gone, of course, and probably made a fortune, selling the lease, good luck to them. And so have the check tablecloths and the low prices, but the food's still pretty good.'

It was not only pretty good, as Richard knew, but excellent and extremely expensive.

'Suits me,' he said.

'Can you get away now, or shall I hang around for a bit?' Jerome seemed anxious to be totally accommodating. 'I'll be quite happy browsing around here.'

'I can go any time you like,' Richard said.

'And how do you feel about walking? It's no distance and it's turned out a lovely morning.'

'Let's walk, then.'

'Good.

They walked together into Farcet Street.

The July day was as sunny as the early mistiness had promised. Heat struck up at them from the pavements. Women were in summer dresses, with their arms bare and with an air of pleasure about them at the comfort of their clothes and at being able to look far prettier than they usually could in this climate.

'Had your holiday yet?' Jerome asked as he and Richard walked along.

'No, not yet,' Richard said. 'Have you?'

Jerome shook his head. 'I'm thinking of taking a fortnight in September. We'll probably go to Cornwall. I've had my bellyful of foreign travel recently. A conference in Ottawa in May, a week of talk and time wasted in Rome last month, and I've probably got to go to Tokyo in November. So a couple of weeks of doing nothing in Cornwall strikes me as about the best sort of holiday to have.'

'You scientists do seem to get around,' Richard said.

'Richard, d'you know, it's years since I've thought of calling myself a scientist,' Jerome said. 'But let's not get started on that. I didn't ask you to lunch to treat you to a load of bloody old might-have-beens. And to be quite honest with you, I like my job. I'm good at it, as Jeannie told you, I know that, and that's a thing in which there's always satisfaction, whereas, if I'd stuck to research, I'd never have been anything but second-rate and should have been miserable.' He paused for a moment, then added, 'Like poor old Clyro.'

At the Europa they had martinis, Jerome recommended the *pâté maison* and the *veau roulé*, and ordered a *Château Gruaud Larose*. The long, narrow room was beginning to fill up and it was very warm, but they were close to the open window.

'Talking of Clyro,' Jerome went on presently, then paused for a long time, spreading *pâté* on his toast. His tone became rather solemn. 'Richard, I don't want to talk out of turn. I mean, I don't want to ask anything you might find awkward. But there's something on which – well, I know it's going to sound stupid when I tell you what it is – but still, the fact is, there's something on which I'd immensely value your opinion.'

Richard could not think of any opinion of his which it required an expensive lunch to purchase. If Jerome and Jeannie had some old books stuck away in their flat which they thought might be valuable, they had only to bring them along to the shop to ask him about them.

'Anything I can . . . ' he said.

Jerome tasted the mouthful of wine that the waiter poured into his glass and took his time over it before he nodded.

'It's like this,' he said. 'You met Hazel last night. You seemed to take to her. Took her home, didn't you? Well now, the thing is this . . . ' The pink of his fleshy cheeks deepened a little, as if he were embarrassed by what he intended to say. 'You know, it was Jeannie's idea that I should talk to you. She said you and Hazel seemed obviously to understand one another, and as I remember you, you always were a perceptive sort of chap.'

'Well?' Richard said.

'Oh hell, it's so difficult to say this sort of thing! What I want to know is whether Hazel said or did anything that struck you as not absolutely – well, I mean a bit unbalanced. And before you answer, let me assure you that she's a very dear friend of Jeannie's and mine and I've only brought the subject up because we're both damnably worried about her.'

After a slight hesitation, Richard said, 'She struck me as a very intelligent woman.'

'Oh, she is, she is,' Jerome said. 'Highly intelligent. Excellent brain. Great charm too, when she's got over her shyness. She's immensely shy, you know. But a delightful person. Which makes it all the more upsetting. If Jeannie and I are right, that's to say.'

'What's put it into your mind?' Richard asked.

'Just little things she says from time to time,' Jerome said. 'Things you can hardly put your finger on. Like sitting in the car with you and looking behind her all the time and seeming to lose track of what you were talking about. And once, just recently, the three of us were going to the theatre together and we'd got out of our taxi and were crossing the pavement, when she stood stock still, looking pale as a ghost, and said, "There – didn't you see him?" – or words to that effect. And Jeannie said, "Who?" And Hazel said, "Oh, nobody." But she was still quite white and she'd started to shake and halfway through the show she suddenly said she wasn't feeling well and had better go home. And there've been one or two other things of the same sort.'

'All as if she felt she was being followed?'

'That's it.'

'And you don't feel it could possibly be true that she is.'

'Well, good God, Richard, a girl like Hazel . . . !'

'But weren't she and her husband involved in the Wolsingham business?' Richard said. 'Real cloak-and-dagger stuff.'

Jerome laid his knife down, sat back in his chair and looked at Richard with an air of heavy sadness.

'I really didn't think you'd say that,' he said. 'A witch-hunter. I never thought you'd come to that.'

'I'm not a witch-hunter,' Richard said. 'It just struck me that if a girl who's been connected with a thing like that thinks she's being followed, just possibly she is. I'd as soon think that as that her mind's cracking up.'

'Yes, of course, if you put it like that . . . But she's gone through a very rough time, you know. A breakdown wouldn't be surprising.'

'What's the story about her husband?' Richard asked. 'I know he's the man who found Wolsingham dead, and that after a year or so he vanished, but that's all.'

'That's about all anyone knows for sure.' Jerome frowned and fumbled with his wine-glass, as if he did not want to be questioned on the subject.

'Did you know him?' Richard went on.

'Oh yes, quite well.'

'Was it a shock when he vanished, or had you half been expecting something to happen?'

'It was a hell of a shock. Then afterwards Jeannie and I felt we ought to have seen it coming – I mean, seen *something* coming, if you understand me. You see, Paul believed everyone thought he'd known all about Wolsingham's activities. Which would have meant, of course, that he'd been in on them too, though there was never a shred of evidence produced against him. Personally, I've always been absolutely certain Paul was dead innocent. He worked under Wolsingham, and he hero-worshipped him, as a number of other people I could name did too. Wolsingham was that kind of man. A virologist – absolutely brilliant. He inspired people, made them think they were a whole lot more brilliant than they were, and I suppose had the knack of bringing out the best in them. I, as it happened, couldn't stand him. An insidious sort of bastard, I always thought, basically arrogant and out for himself, using that skill he had with people just for his own advancement. But then, I never worked with him. I wasn't exposed to that mind of his day after day. I just met him a few times on various committees, where you could always count on him making a damned nuisance of himself. He always wanted to feel sure he was getting just a bit more than the next chap. But to Paul he was the sun around which the planets revolved. Odd, you know, I don't think I've ever felt like that about anybody – perhaps

Jeannie excepted.' Jerome gave a self-conscious laugh. 'But at least that's normal.'

'Are you suggesting that the relationship between Wolsingham and Clyro wasn't normal?' Richard asked.

'Sexually, you mean? Oh lord, no. Nothing like that. I never knew much about Wolsingham's private life, though I heard all the rumours, of course. In my job you do. I heard all about his women and his illegitimates. I don't know how much of it was true. Stories like that always snowball, once they begin. But what I do know is that Paul was utterly devoted to Hazel. I doubt if he knew any other woman existed. I really believe that, in spite of what happened.'

'In spite of his walking out and leaving her.'

'If that's what he did.'

Richard looked thoughtfully at the troubled face of the man beside him. It was utterly unlike the lean, excitable face of the young man whom Richard had known years ago, yet somewhere behind the pink, smooth covering, he felt, that other face must be lurking. We never wholly shed anything that we have ever been.

'If it's Mrs Clyro you want to talk about,' Richard said, 'hadn't we better go back to the beginning?'

'Yes. All right.' Jerome kneaded the table napkin on his knees between his rather large hands. 'Well, you seem to know about Wolsingham. He was in charge of that research station near Overscaig in Sutherland. A desolate sort of life, I should think, miles from anywhere. And it was all wildly secret stuff they were doing there. Viruses and so on that could wipe out the whole population of Europe. Not the sort of thing you were allowed to talk about to anybody, not even your wife. Incidentally, can you think of a worse sort of hell in marriage than that? I mean, spending your day doing something you couldn't even grumble about to your wife in the evenings. If I couldn't go home and spill all my grouses on to Jeannie, I'd go mad. Luckily for me, she's wonderfully discreet. She can talk a blue streak, but she never says a single thing she shouldn't.'

Jerome looked curiously pathetic as he said it, and it occurred to Richard, though he could not have said why it should have done so just then, that some people put on fat when they are unhappy.

'Well, as I said,' Jerome went on, 'Wolsingham was in charge and Paul worked with him, more closely, I suppose, than anyone else. And he and Hazel had a croft in the village near the place and seemed to love the life. They'd only been married a year or so, and when I met them there for the first time, which was when I was on some CPS round of inspection, they seemed to me two perfectly radiant young people, glorying in each other and the life they were leading among the sheep and the heather and the golden eagles and whatnot.' He coughed. 'Sorry, I don't want to sound emotional about it, but what came later was so bloody upsetting, so – so absolutely unforeseeable. First Wolsingham took that hefty dose of potassium cyanide. Horrible, but quick and absolutely certain. And it happened to be Paul who went in and found him. He went into the lab late one evening to see to some work of his own, saw Wolsingham's lights on – apparently not many people commit suicide in the dark, isn't that interesting? – and went in to ask him about something and found him stone dead. And after that it came out that Wolsingham had been slipping information to the Russians about the work of the Institute for years, and that our security people had been just about to pounce on him. And he couldn't face that, so he did himself in.'

'I remember most of that,' Richard said.

'And that's where the Clyro story really begins, as far as Jeannie and I are concerned,' Jerome continued. 'One day Paul came to see me in London. He told me he was afraid of going right round the bend if he had to stay on at Overscaig. I suppose he picked on me to confide in because we'd seemed to hit it off very well when we met in Scotland. As a matter of fact, in some ways he reminded me of you, a quiet, withdrawn sort of chap, with a lot of warmth under the surface, if you could get at it. He told me it wasn't only that he'd come to loathe the work he was doing – its destructiveness and that frightful secrecy I was telling you about, not at all a normal atmosphere for a healthy-minded young scientist to work in – but he'd got it into his head that everyone who knew him thought he'd been in with Wolsingham and would have been in gaol if he hadn't been clever about destroying evidence. And for all I know, he was right – I mean, that that's the sort of attitude he kept running into. There's no platitude people are more willing to believe than that you can't touch pitch without being defiled. Guilt by association and all that. I'm not sure I hadn't some suspicion of him myself until I got to know him better.'

'And then?'

'Then I did some looking into things and pulled a few strings and got him a job with the Blofield Research Institute near Cambridge. All plain agricultural stuff, without a secret in any one of their files. He and Hazel were delighted, got themselves a beautiful little cottage, thatch, oak beams and everything, and seemed all set for a new beginning. And then the old thing started up again. Or so Paul said. Hazel insisted it was mostly imagination. Jeannie and I were beginning to know them fairly well by then. They came to London quite often to the theatre and so on, and used to spend the night with us, and we'd go and stay with them occasionally in the cottage. Hazel and Jeannie got on wonderfully well from the start. Which is partly why I'm telling you all this stuff now. Hazel's so appallingly alone, you see. I sometimes get the feeling that Jeannie and I are the only friends she's got.'

The *veau roulé* had come and most of it had gone.

Richard said, 'By "the old thing" you mean the belief that Clyro had been in with Wolsingham.'

Jerome nodded. 'He began to be as unhappy as he'd been at Overscaig and asked me if I couldn't help him get a job somewhere else, perhaps abroad. He talked about Australia. There wasn't much I could do for him in that line and I suggested he might be better off in industry. A university would have suited him best, of course. Not such a tight little circle as a research station. There's just as much gossip, naturally, but it's more diluted, so to speak, simply because the numbers are so much larger. But it's difficult to get into a university if you haven't gone step by step up the academic ladder. And Paul wasn't all that brilliant. Working with Wolsingham, he'd been making quite a name for himself, but on his own he obviously wasn't anything outstanding. The world's full of his kind. They make wonderful assistants to the really able men, but there's some spark lacking. So, as I said, I suggested industry. And then he vanished.'

'From this place, Blofield?'

'From his home, actually. He left home one Saturday morning to go to his work, just as usual, but apparently never got there. Since it was a Saturday, when a lot of people didn't turn up to work anyhow, nobody in the Institute gave it a thought. And when he didn't come home for lunch, Hazel didn't worry much either, because he was always a bit casual about turning up at the right time for meals, if he happened to get engrossed in what he was doing. She only began to worry towards evening, and didn't get in touch with the police until quite late that night.'

'Didn't they find out anything?'

'Not a single damned thing. Of course they picked up endless information that he'd been seen in almost every part of the country, but none of it led to anything. From that day to this not one thing has been seen or heard of Paul Clyro. My guess is that the police, knowing the background of his story, wrote it off early as a suicide and didn't work extra hard at finding anything out.'

'Don't suicides usually leave notes behind them?'

'Usually, not invariably.'

'What about his having slipped behind the Iron Curtain?'

Jerome gave a distressed sigh. 'I've tried to make it plain, Richard, that I'm absolutely certain Paul was dead innocent. He admired Wolsingham, he depended on him, he believed he was about the greatest thing walking the earth, but he never understood the first thing about him. I think the real shock for Paul, when he found Wolsingham dead, wasn't just the normal shock anyone would feel at stumbling over a dead body, but the discovery afterwards that Wolsingham was a traitor. I think it was that that more or less unhinged Paul. If your God betrays you, you tend not to have much faith left in yourself, don't you?'

'You're calling Clyro unhinged now,' Richard said. 'I thought it was his wife you were worrying about.'

'Well, yes, that's what I'm *worrying* about,' Jerome agreed. 'I've stopped worrying about Paul now. It all happened a couple of years ago, and I don't suppose any of us will ever know the truth about it. As I said, he walked out of the house that Saturday morning without taking any clothes with him, or more than a very little money – just the change he had in his pockets, Hazel said. And that was that . . . It *is* Hazel I'm worrying about now. Jeannie and I have stood by, watching what all this has done to her, and we're worrying like hell about her.'

'Because she seems to think she's being followed about?'

'That's the main thing, yes.'

Richard crumbled some bread, looking at the pieces piercingly, as if, like tea-leaves in a cup, they might have some meaning for him.

He said, 'I suppose Clyro wasn't by any chance a bald man, was he?'

Chapter Three

'*Bald?*' Jerome said.

'Yes.'

'In God's name, why bald?'

'Well, was he?' Richard asked.

'No, as a matter of fact he had rather thick hair, which he wore rather long.'

'What colour?'

'A sort of mid-brown.'

'I suppose he could have gone bald in two years, couldn't he?'

Jerome wrinkled his forehead, looking extremely bewildered. 'I suppose so. It doesn't seem likely, somehow. He was quite a young man, you know. About the same age as Hazel.' He repeated, 'Why?'

'Just an idea,' Richard said. 'It doesn't sound as if there's anything in it. That time at the theatre, Jerome, when she seemed to think she was being followed by someone, didn't it occur to you that it could have been Clyro she'd seen in the crowd?'

'It's funny you should say that,' Jerome answered. 'Jeannie had that idea. We discussed it afterwards. But you know, if he had been there, I somehow think she or I would have seen him. He was a tallish man. It wouldn't be easy for him to disappear in a crowd. So it would have been odd if we'd both missed him. But we did think perhaps Hazel *thought* she saw him. It's quite easy to do that if you've someone very much on your mind. I remember when I first met Jeannie I used to keep seeing her everywhere, and then when the other woman got close I'd realize there wasn't even any real resemblance.'

'But that evening at the theatre was when you began to think Mrs Clyro was going mental.'

Jerome stirred uneasily on his chair and said nothing.

'Well, where do I come in?' Richard asked. 'Just what do you want me to do?'

'Oh, I don't want you to *do* anything,' Jerome said. 'I don't want you to be bothered with the problem. I just wanted your opinion. Is she – well, ill or not? Did she do anything yesterday evening to make you suspect she was? You see, we've got this feeling of responsibility about her. I can't say why, exactly, except that that's how she's always affected us. It's something to do with that aloneness of hers. While Paul was with her I think their friends were mostly his friends, and when he went off and they all started falling away, she hadn't anybody.'

Richard remembered that Hazel Clyro had spoken of Jerome as a good man, a kind one.

Jerome went on, 'You've seen what she's like at a party. She sits by herself unless someone makes a point of talking to her. You can't draw her into things in the ordinary way. I think myself she's never made an effort to get over Paul's disappearance.'

'I suppose the fact that perhaps she'll never be certain if he's alive or dead makes it extra hard,' Richard said.

'Yes, I imagine she keeps on half-hoping all the time.'

'What's your own theory about what happened to him?'

'All in all, I think there was some kind of accident,' Jerome said. 'I can't see him doing anything as cruel, without any cause at all, as walking out on her and leaving her without a word of explanation. He was quite an imaginative sort of man, he'd have known what it would do to her. For the same reason, I can't see him going off to commit suicide without leaving a letter behind him. But suppose he was killed that morning, walking to work, by a hit-and-run driver. I'm only guessing, of course. As I was saying, there was never any trace of evidence.'

'But the police would have found the body if something like that had happened.'

'Not if the driver panicked, thought he'd been seen, perhaps recognized, in the neighbourhood, so put the body in the car and dumped it somewhere a long way off . . . if it had been a lorry or a van, that wouldn't have been difficult.'

Richard was pursuing the crumbs of his bread again, pushing them into a kind of pattern.

'Did anyone ever suggest murder?'

'Oh, of course. There were people who were sure some of Wolsingham's friends had come after Paul and finished him off because he knew too much.'

'But you never thought so.'

'As I've said before,' Jerome exclaimed with exasperation, 'I don't think he knew anything! And Wolsingham's friends would have known that, wouldn't they? It would have been an utterly pointless murder.'

'Pointless murders are not unknown.'

Jerome gazed at Richard for a moment with a look of anxiety, then tried to do a little more explaining. 'Jeannie and I aren't just busybodies, Richard. We're honestly fond of Hazel and we want to help her. But it's difficult saying to one of your friends, "Look here, I think you're going round the bend and ought to see a doctor." And that's what somebody ought to say to her if she goes on seeing people who aren't there. I mean, even if it's true that a person's on the edge of a breakdown, it isn't just the easiest thing in the world to make them do something about it. And if it weren't true, and one went blundering into something one didn't understand, then they'd lose every scrap of trust they had in one, wouldn't they?'

'So, if I see her again, you want a sort of progress report.'

'That sounds a bit awful. But – yes – that's it, I suppose, though of course only if you feel it might be helpful.'

Richard had not completely made up his mind at that time whether or not he wanted to see Hazel Clyro again. Or he thought that he had not. He thought that he was still free to choose between ringing her up and simply omitting to do so. He had not reckoned with the hidden compulsions in his own nature, which that evening would settle the problem for him in the simplest fashion, making him open the telephone directory and find her number and dial it, his fingers moving with a jerky, nervous eagerness, at the very moment when he had been telling himself that he would like a chat on the telephone with Anne. He often had lengthy telephone talks with Anne fairly late in the evenings, when her children and her mother had all gone up to bed, and he himself, after dinner with Harriet and Bernard, was alone in his top floor flat. It made an agreeably calming end of the day, particularly if he happened to be suffering from an overdose of Harriet's advice, freely offered, on everything that affected him.

He had had a large overdose of it that night at dinner in the high Victorian dining-room downstairs, a room which contrived to be a comfortable place in which to eat well-cooked if rather solid plain food, in spite of its being hideously furnished in fumed oak with loudly coloured, angularly patterned curtains and carpet. Perhaps unwisely, he had told Harriet and Bernard about his lunch with Jerome and the moment that he had finished, Harriet had said sharply, 'Don't!'

'Don't what?' Richard had asked.

'Don't have anything to do with that woman. It isn't only that you won't be able to help her, which you won't, because nobody can help anybody who doesn't want to help themselves, and it doesn't sound as if she does. But she's absolutely and completely wrong for you.'

'How d'you know? You've never met her.'

'I do know.'

'You can't know.' Even after sharing a house with Harriet and Bernard for ten years Richard had never entirely accustomed himself to the things that Harriet knew with that utter, unshakeable certainty.

She sighed with impatience at his stupidity and said, 'It's as I was saying this morning, she's another of those women who'll turn out to be eternally faithful to someone who's dead and gone, or married, or otherwise unattainable. They're the only ones you ever bother about seriously. And as I've told you again and again, they're so bad for you, Richard, really so dreadfully bad. Not that that's the situation with Anne, of course, but that's how you see it, and if you woke up to the truth that she'd marry you tomorrow, you'd only panic and cut her right out of your life. No, of course you mustn't see any more of the Clyro woman.'

The eyes of Richard and Bernard met for a moment and Bernard gave a faint smile. He himself would not have been affected, one way or the other, by Harriet's opinion, but would have remained quietly inattentive while the tide washed over him, and in the end done what he liked. And she, oddly enough, would have been aware of this and would not have minded it. In fact, she really liked never having to be held answerable for anything she advised. But Richard had a streak of contrariness in him which made it practically certain that the first thing that he would do on going up to his flat would be to telephone Hazel Clyro.

Actually, it was not quite the first thing that he did. Before it, he opened the window wide and stood leaning on the windowsill for some minutes, looking out at the summer dusk. The street overlooked by the window was a wide one, with old plane trees standing at intervals along the pavements. The street lamps between them had just been lit up and sharpened the shadows cast by the trees. The evening was still nearly as hot as the day had been and from all the open windows of the tall houses came a chattering of voices and occasional bursts of laughter or clapping from television sets, and a faint background of music.

Harriet was far from right about Richard, he did not yearn only after women who were unattainable. At different times he had yearned with astonishing intensity after women who had turned out to be most satisfactorily attainable and with one or two of whom he had had relationships of depth and importance. It had just happened that he had not let Harriet know about them. He had not wanted her to lay those kind but heavy hands of hers upon them. Yet up to a point she was right concerning him, for always, in the end, something in his feeling for Anne had seemed to modify what he was able to feel for any other woman.

He turned away from the window. Pouring some whisky into a tumbler, he went to the kitchen for water to add to it, then stretched himself out full-length on the sofa, sipped his drink and after a few minutes reached for the telephone directory.

It was at his elbow, on a coffee table made of yew tree, a very plain, pleasant, modern little coffee table. All the furniture in the room was modern, simple and of light-coloured woods. The effect on Richard of spending his time among old books in a twilight of leather and parchment and dim gold lettering, was to make him want his home to be as different as possible. Only the Curtis flower prints on the walls had not been created during the last ten years.

A moment later he dialled Hazel Clyro's number.

She answered almost at once, 'Hazel Clyro speaking.'

It was a bad line and her voice sounded faint and remote.

'This is Richard Hedon,' he said.

He paused to give her a chance to show whether or not this fact gave her any pleasure. There was silence.

He went on, 'After yesterday I wanted to know, I wondered . . .'

As he hesitated once more, she said, 'You wanted to know if I'd seen him again. Well, no, I haven't. But then, I haven't been out. I rang them up at the office to say I had a touch of flu. It was untrue. I haven't. It isn't the right time of year for flu, and anyway I almost never get it. But I felt it would be a comforting sort of thing to have, so normal and ordinary. I don't like seeing him, you know. Whenever I do, I always tell them at the office I'm ill. I expect they really think I drink in secret and go ill when I've got a hangover. As they all do it too, it doesn't worry them.'

'I wondered,' Richard said, 'if we could meet again.'

'I wonder at your wanting to,' she said.

'Why shouldn't I?'

'Because of that farcical end to the evening.'

'I didn't think it was farcical.'

'You took it seriously? You didn't think I was putting on an act simply to stimulate your interest in me? That's what I'd have thought in your place.'

He did not want to tell her of all the different things that he had thought.

35

'Will you have dinner with me?' he asked. 'Tomorrow or the day after?'

'Oh, I can easily manage tomorrow,' she said. 'I'm always free. And thank you – I mean, for not minding the things I see.'

They arranged where and when to meet the next evening.

It was the beginning for Richard of a period of obsession.

Even at the time, he realized that a good deal of it had little to do with Hazel herself. Away from parties, she turned out to be a pleasantly friendly woman with whom to spend an evening, detached, undemanding, ready to fall in with any plans he suggested. It was true that occasionally she had moods of silence, and if he tried to bring her out of them, reacted with perhaps excessive nervous irritability, and sometimes she cancelled a meeting without offering any excuse. But if he had not seen her once in helpless terror at the appearance of a bald-headed man who happened to be passing in a grey Cortina, he would never for one moment have worried about her sanity. It was the question of his own that slightly disturbed him.

He knew himself well enough to understand that his relationship with Hazel was a kind of repetition of his relationship with Anne, and that this was a very important factor in it, particularly as there was the possibility of a different outcome. For Paul Clyro was not Peter Damerel. He had not died, fighting for his life and with his hand in Anne's, of cancer of the liver. Clyro had left his wife abruptly, callously, escaping the problems of his own dubious past and leaving her to carry the burden alone, with nothing explained. That, at least, seemed probable, unless you went along with Jerome in believing that there had been some fantastic element of accident in his disappearance. If you did not believe this, Paul Clyro surely was the sort of man with whom you could successfully compete. And if you found that you could, perhaps it was really the shade of Peter Damerel to whom you were at last standing up, and perhaps this was not exactly fair to Hazel, since it was not really treating her as herself, a separate individual.

But still, for Richard there was a profound excitement in the situation and a haunting sense of promise. During the next few weeks he never seemed to be entirely free of her presence. She seemed to be somewhere near him all the time, just out of sight, yet making him feel, in the middle of a day's work, that he could turn and talk to her at any moment. His mind was almost never wholly, undividedly on any other subject. Whether he had seen her recently, or was soon about to do so, she constantly occupied some part of his attention. It was not totally unlike anything that he had experienced before, except in degree. In that it was unique. Obsession, and he did not like the thought, was the only word for it.

Anne knew that he was seeing Hazel frequently and seemed to be pleased about it. In fact, he began to wonder if it had not been simply so that he should meet Hazel that Anne had insisted on taking him to the Ottershaws' party. She sometimes spoke as if she had brought him and Hazel together deliberately, guessing how he would respond to the other woman. Had she perhaps done it in order to be free at last of the limited claims that he made upon Anne herself?

There was no end to the questions that you could ask yourself about a situation of the kind once you started.

When he saw Hazel, she continued to talk very little about herself. At times, as when Richard had first seen her, she seemed near to talking about Paul Clyro, but then always shied away from the subject. If Richard had not already known as much about her as he did, he would have found her irritatingly uncommunicative. As things were, he thought that he understood this in her and that if he went very carefully, the barrier would one day break of itself.

It did, but not in any way that he had expected.

She liked to spend their evenings together at the theatre, or at concerts or at the cinema. She very seldom seemed to want to be exposed to the risk of anything as personal as two or three hours of mere dining together, talking, and perhaps going home to her flat or his. Although he had often driven her to her home, he had never been invited into it, and she had always shaken her head at the suggestion that they might go back to the flat in St John's Wood. A quiet two or three hours sitting side by side watching something happen on a stage or a screen seemed to give her pleasure, but for the two of them to come closer together than that seemed to be something that she still wanted to avoid at all costs.

Then one evening they went to see a film called *Pardon Me For Dying*.

Hazel enjoyed thriller films and that it was a thriller that had been running for some weeks and been exceptionally well reviewed as an almost serious film was all that Richard knew about it. It was on in one of the Leicester Square cinemas, and as they were having dinner in Old Compton Street the cinema was only a few minutes' walk away.

When Richard suggested that they should go to see it, Hazel smiled and said, 'That's just what I'd like. You're beginning to understand me at last. The fact is, in case you haven't noticed it, I'm a rather dull woman with shocking taste. Thank you for putting up with me.'

She was looking anything but dull that evening. She was wearing a high-necked, sleeveless dress of rough black silk, with a necklace of chains of gold, silver and copper. Her coppery hair was loose on her shoulders. She had eaten and drunk more than usual and looked relaxed and contented. Richard felt proud of himself, because he believed that he was the cause of a considerable change in her.

They went to the cinema, to front seats in the Circle.

Unfortunately they had arrived just as the earlier showing of the film was ending. There was a good deal of shooting, the sound of stampeding feet, some angular shadows of running men showing on a white background, then a shot of a body spreadeagled on an expanse of snow, with a revolver a few inches from an outflung hand. Then there was some music and that was that.

Hazel settled herself comfortably into her seat and said, 'It looks promising, doesn't it? I like lots of shooting. Can you shoot, Richard?'

'The only time I ever tried, the kick of the thing nearly knocked me over backwards,' he answered.

'Have you ever killed anything?'

'I've set mousetraps and done a little fishing.'

'Bloodthirsty Richard,' she mocked him mildly. 'I only hope this doesn't go psychological on us. I've no use for the kind of film where all the characters turn out to be all one person really, good, bad, and all the rest of it – you know what I mean.

38

What I really like are people who all snarl at one another out of the corners of their mouths, and do several nice, straight-forward murders, then chase each other over roof-tops.'

Her laugh was quiet and gentle.

They watched the news and a short documentary about the mating habits of seagulls. Then *Pardon Me For Dying* began again.

It was while the credit titles were being shown that the change came over Hazel. Richard was not concentrating on the screen. The names on it, as they slid by, only evoked in him a casual thought about what extraordinary names some people have, particularly those involved in film-making – Winella Drushki, Marti Sunnuck, Ohna Febelshoxen – and he noticed the name of the novel from which the film had been adapted, *Taken As Red*, by someone called Gavin Chilmark, of whom Richard had never heard. Then he saw Hazel suddenly lean forward in her seat, clasping both hands to her stomach, and begin to gasp.

Richard felt the flood of panic which anyone feels when a companion is taken violently ill. Seriously ill, perhaps. In the half-light of the cinema, reflected from the screen, he could see Hazel's face, contorted with pain.

He made a quick grab at her hand.

'What's happened? What's the matter? Shall we leave?'

The woman who was sitting on the other side of Hazel whispered to her, 'Oh dear, is something wrong? What is it? Can I help?'

Hazel drew some long shuddering breaths, let her head droop forward for a moment, then sat back once more.

'I'm sorry,' she answered the woman. 'There's nothing wrong. I – I just thought I'd dropped something.'

Her hand was rigid in Richard's and her face was stiffly empty.

'Are you sure?' the woman asked uncertainly.

'Yes, really – just something from my handbag. I'll look for it later.' Hazel's voice was quiet and normal. Turning to Richard, she went on in a whisper, 'I'm quite all right. I just had a bit of a shock. I'm sorry if I startled you. It was stupid of me.'

'What shock?' Richard asked, all of a sudden dreading to hear her say something about having seen a bald-headed man in the cinema.

'The title of that novel,' she said. 'Did you notice it?'

'*Taken As Red.*' And that meant, of course, it struck Richard, that this must be a spy film, and it had not been specially tactful of him to bring the wife of Paul Clyro to see it.

With a shaky sigh, she said, 'I thought so.'

Someone behind them said, 'Sh!'

Richard still had hold of her hand, which felt cold now as well as rigid.

'Wouldn't you like to leave?' he asked again.

'No,' she said quickly. 'Oh no, I want to see it. I want to, I – must.' He felt her give an abrupt shiver, then she withdrew her hand from his. 'I'll explain afterwards. But now I've just got to see it through.'

'Sh!' said the voice behind them once more.

Hazel and Richard subsided into silence.

The film was a good one of its kind, taut, fast-moving, at times really sinister, but with a conventional plot about a man who knew something that he did not know he knew, and with nothing specially remarkable about it that Richard could discern. Hazel, he could sense, remained abnormally tense from beginning to end, and when they were leaving the cinema was silent and looked far away, lost in her own thoughts. She hardly spoke at all on the way out to her home, to which Richard drove her as usual.

But then, as she unlocked her door, she said, 'Would you like to come in, Richard?'

He followed her in. He noticed that she walked stiffly, as if she were still suffering from shock. The light that fell on her face in the little hall showed her cheeks as drawn and colourless. By contrast, her eyes looked burningly alive, but what emotion had kindled the fire in them Richard could not guess. It could have been fear, hope, love, hate, or a mixture of all of them.

She took him into the sitting-room that he had never seen. It was a disappointing room cheaply and impersonally furnished, and dusty too, as if she did not care enough about anything there to look after it. Perhaps, Richard thought, she had taken the flat furnished and this stuff did not belong to her. As he had thought when he had had his first glimpse of her hall, it was no setting for her.

As soon as she had turned on the light, she crossed to the windows and drew the curtains, then she dropped into a chair, put her face into her hands and began to cry. She cried almost soundlessly, but her whole body shook.

Richard took her by the wrists, pulled her hands away from her face and drew her to her feet. He put his arms round her and held her close to him.

She clung desperately, digging her face hard into his neck, then abruptly lifting her head and putting her mouth against his. There was frenzy in it. He could taste the salt of her tears. But it was not a real kiss, only an impulsive and unsatisfactory experiment, an attempt to find calm. After an instant she twisted free of him, dropped back into the chair and began rubbing her face with her handkerchief.

He said, 'I suppose you haven't any whisky in the house.'

She shook her head.

'Anything else?'

'I think there's some cooking brandy.'

'Where?'

'In the kitchen.'

He found his way to the kitchen and discovered the brandy in one of the cupboards there. Only a very little was gone from the bottle. Hazel would never die of drink whatever other troubles she had. He poured some brandy into a tumbler. The kitchen had the same half-neglected look as the sitting-room, only just stopping short of the squalid. The cupboard shelves were stacked with odds and ends in paper bags. The sink looked greasy. The whole place smelt of frying. Everything seemed to be impregnated with the stale smell of lonely meals of bacon and eggs, of chops, of sausages. Was it just that Hazel was a thoroughly undomesticated woman, he wondered, whose home would always be like this, or was it that when Paul Clyro left her, she had simply lost heart? He carried the glass of brandy to the sitting-room.

She drank a little, made a face and said, 'It's horrible.'

Richard did not doubt that it was, but at least her tears stopped. He waited. She drank a little more and her breathing grew steadier.

After a moment she said, 'There's something I want to tell you, Richard.'

'Take your time,' he said. 'There's no hurry.'

'It's about that film, *Taken As Red*.'

'The film was called *Pardon Me For Dying*.'

She gave an impatient frown. 'I mean the book, the one it was made from. That was called *Taken As Red*, wasn't it?'

'Do you remember the name of the man who wrote it?'

'I don't think so. It was Gavin Something.'

'You didn't notice?'

'Not really. I know I'd never heard of him.'

'Yes.'

'I didn't notice either. I just saw, *Taken As Red* and sort of blacked out with shock. I know you don't understand why it was a shock. I'm going to tell you. But the writer's name, I hoped you'd have noticed it.'

'It would be easy enough to find out, if it's important to you,' Richard said. 'But why *is* it important?'

'Because he's my husband,' she said. 'He's Paul.'

Her crying started afresh.

It took longer to quieten her this time. Richard did not press any more brandy on her, or touch her or speak to her, but left her to deal with the spasm herself.

After a little while she gave an exhausted sigh and stretched out in her chair. She began to speak in the tone of a person who has a story all rehearsed, because she has told it to herself over and over again, yet tells it aloud at last with extreme reluctance.

'All my life I've really only loved one man,' she said. 'I want you to know that, Richard, because it's been seeming to me as if – well, as if, perhaps, if you didn't realize that, you might get hurt. And I should hate that. I like you so much. You've been so good to me.'

A great consolation prize. Richard felt his features stiffen slightly.

'Good to you – like Jerome,' he suggested.

'Not at all like Jerome. He's been very kind and very practical and he and Jeannie have done a great deal to help me. But you've got imagination. Otherwise I don't think I'd risk telling you what I'm going to now. I know I shan't tell it to Jerome. Or not until I've thought it out very carefully. He won't believe me, for one thing, until he's got all sorts of corroboration. And when he gets it, he'll talk sober, solid sense to me. And that isn't what I happen to want tonight. So you won't do it either, will you? Not tonight. Promise?'

'Go ahead.'

'I simply couldn't stand it,' she said. 'Not after a shock like that. Not after suddenly finding out in that awful way that Paul's alive. *Taken As Red* . . . You see, that's the title of a book Paul and I were going to write together.'

'Now just one minute – ' Richard began, then realized that what he had been about to say sounded altogether too like the sober, solid sense with which he had been challenged not to respond to her. 'The book?' he said, and left it at that.

She smiled. 'I know what you were going to say, and it was nice of you not to. You were going to say a title like that is just a pun that anyone could have thought of. You were going to say it's sheer accident that a Gavin Somebody thought of it and wrote a book and managed to sell it to a film company and have a film made of it and probably got lots of money from it. Lucky Gavin. Lucky, lucky Gavin – whose real name, you see, happens to be Paul Clyro. Oh yes – ' Richard had been about to speak, but her hand shot out checking him. 'Oh yes,' she said, 'because we did more than just think of a title. Once we began, we couldn't stop. Living in that world, among all those people, just bristling with secrets, it was so easy to make up a spy story about them all. We used to sit together over drinks in the evening – I used to drink quite a lot in those days – working out the yarn and having a wonderful time. But we couldn't agree how the story was to end. I wanted a tragic ending, I thought it suited the story, and Paul wanted a happy one. He always wanted happy endings. He couldn't face pain. That's what he ran away from, of course. Just being hurt by the looks on people's faces. But that plot of ours was the plot of the film we saw this evening. It wasn't just the title, it was

43

the whole plot.' Her voice rose as if she were expecting Richard to contradict her. 'It was, it was! From beginning to end I knew what was coming next. Paul wrote that book. And that means he's alive and I'm going to find him! He's hidden from me for two years, but now I'm going to find him and make him face me, and face everyone else too, and be himself again!'

Chapter Four

Hazel stayed sitting limply in her chair, her face drained of colour, distraught and tear-stained. She was not at all beautiful just then. Yet Richard felt something for her that he had not felt before. It was a sharp, unhappy emotion, and it took him a moment to recognize it as jealousy. He was not much given to jealousy as a rule, but now it made a rough, jagged wound in his consciousness. Alive or dead, he hated Paul Clyro, and half-hated Hazel herself because the man mattered so much to her still that the thought of him could reduce her to this damp, exhausted wreck of a woman.

After a moment he said, 'Suppose you're right . . . '

'I am!' she said. 'You needn't look at me in that pitying way. I know I'm right.'

Richard had not been aware that he had been looking pitying, since pity was only a very small part of the harsh and complicated thing that he was feeling.

'I was going to say,' he said, 'suppose you're right, are you sure you want him back?'

'Why shouldn't I?' she asked.

'I didn't say you shouldn't. I only wondered, have you thought out what it means if he's alive and wrote that book?'

She wrinkled her forehead. 'I haven't had time to work everything out. What does it mean?'

'It means that he isn't a poor, sick man who wandered away from you, half out of his mind, lost and alone, and still needing you to help him take up a respected place in life again. In fact, he's doing very nicely, thank you. He's writing successful thrillers somewhere, and being paid large sums for having them made into films, and not getting in touch with you to tell you the good news, or sending you any of the nice money.'

She looked at him vacantly, then said, 'It doesn't sound like you to say anything so cruel.'

'I didn't mean to be cruel.' Yet probably he had. And cruel or not, he thought, this was what she needed rather than a too easy sympathy. 'I was just pointing out to you an obvious fact.'

'And you're quite right, of course. But I've still got to find him. For my own sake as much as for his. Can't you understand that? And if it turns out that he's happy and successful and that he walked out on me simply because he didn't want me any more . . . ' She stopped.

'Well?' Richard said.

'Well,' she said after a pause, 'at least I'll know where I am.' Her face became almost tranquil. 'I'll know what it is I've got to accept.'

'Will you divorce him?'

'I don't know whether or not I'd bother.'

'But aren't you ever going to want to marry again?'

She managed a faint smile. 'Didn't I begin this by telling you there was only one man I'd loved in all my life?'

'But if he turns out to be not the man you thought he was?'

'He won't.'

'But if he does.'

'Then how could I ever trust myself to love anyone else?'

'That's a counsel of despair if ever I heard one.'

'I'm not afraid of despair. I've lived with it for a long time.'

He sat down near her and reached for her hand. 'All right, Hazel. What do you want to do? Can I help somehow, or am I only in the way?'

'Oh, you can help, if you want to,' she answered at once.

'I don't want to at all, but I always will, if you want it.'

'Then tell me how I can find out where he is.'

'Hmmm . . . I suppose that shouldn't be too difficult.'

'It shouldn't, should it? You could find out who published that book, and get his address from the publisher. I'm sure, as you're a bookseller, you could do that quite easily.'

Richard did not mention the fact that books like *Taken As Red* did not find their way on to the shelves of Joseph Hedon and Sons.

'His address may be pretty private,' he said. 'He isn't writing under his own name, remember.'

'But I'm sure you could get it.'

'Anyway, I'll ask around. But you're remembering, aren't you, I might come up with the fact that Gavin What's-his-name isn't your Paul at all?'

'It isn't possible. I can't, I *mustn't* be wrong about him!'

There was such fierce passion in her answer that Richard caught himself thinking with a certain pleasure that after all she had a big score to settle with Paul Clyro, and that it might be for revenge that she wanted to find him, rather than for the rebuilding of her marriage. But as she went on, Richard felt that her brief flare of anger had actually been against him, for reminding her that her guess about the writer of the novel might be mistaken.

'You want me to be wrong, don't you?' she said. 'You don't want to believe me. You're only going to help me to prove to me what a fool I am. But you'll find I'm not wrong, Richard. I've been wrong again and again in my life about all sorts of things, but I'm not wrong this time.'

'You know, I don't think I want you to be wrong,' he said. 'I think I want you to be right, because I see it's the only way of settling things for you. And once it's settled, I don't believe you'll find you're incapable of ever loving anyone else again. But we can come back to that some other time.' He put her hand back on her lap, gave it a pat and stood up. 'As I said, I'll ask around, and I'll let you know as soon as I manage to find out anything.'

He was thinking that the first person to ask was Anne. She was far more closely in touch with the publishing world than he was, and would at least be able to find out without much difficulty if the writer of *Taken As Red* was a man easy to approach or not. She might even know a good deal about him already. In any case, the chances were that a few telephone calls would dig up most of the information that Hazel required.

It was too late when Richard reached home that night to

ring Anne up, but he did so at her office the next morning, and asked if he could drop in on her in the evening.

He was invited to what she called 'a meal of sorts'. This, he knew, would mean a very excellent dinner, cooked by Anne's mother, Mrs Tenbury, but it meant also that the two children would be there and would have to be tolerated. This did not dismay Richard too much. Sarah, aged nine, and Martin, aged seven, were a pleasant, good-natured pair, if disinclined to endure any talk that was over their heads. They had a simple faith that the world revolved around them. Their mother's and their grandmother's, of course, did, so it was natural for the children to take for granted that any visitor who came to the house was also their personal property.

They felt this particularly if they approved of the visitor, as they did of Richard. That evening, immediately after the meal, which was of fried chicken with all the trimmings, followed by strawberries and cream, they took possession of him for a game of racing demon, while Anne and her mother did the washing up. The game became very noisy and exciting. Sarah, who had fair hair and blue eyes, like her father, and looking shyly, vulnerably innocent, played with machine-like speed and precision and won easily. She also won at the game of cheating that followed, looking flustered and guilty when she had the right card to play and airily confident when she had only the wrong one. If she ever graduated to poker, Richard thought, she would be a holy terror.

He himself lost all the games, and not for want of trying. He had long ago lost the illusion that there was any need to play down to these children. Martin played deliberately and carefully, frowning a great deal and showing polite sympathy with Richard for his incompetence. Martin was short for his age, but stocky and muscular, with hair almost as black as his mother's and a slightly sombre air, as if, as the one male in the house, he had already decided to take his responsibilities seriously. It was an air that he appeared to have inherited from his father, even though Martin could not remember him. Peter had had that thoughtfully quiet manner, which even in his moods of gaiety had never quite left him.

His photograph was there, on the top of a bookshelf, looking down at the three of them as they squatted on the hearthrug, with their cards spread out on the coffee table between them. Peter had had a heavy forehead, with straight, formidable brows over remarkably gentle eyes, a strong, rather craggy jaw and a sensitive mouth. It was a face that revealed both sides of his nature, the kind and perceptive man of imagination somehow fused with a man of action.

Richard had always envied Peter his active qualities. In contrast, Richard had always felt himself to be deplorably lacking in them. He had never been athletic, he had never wanted or been able to command other people, he always tended, on the whole, to dodge responsibility. The strong friendship between him and Peter, which had come spontaneously into being as soon as Anne introduced them, had been at least to some extent the attraction of opposites.

When the washing up was finished and the children had been sent away to bed, Mrs Tenbury stayed chatting in the sitting-room for a few minutes, then said that there was a concert that she wanted to listen to on her radio in her room and left Anne and Richard together. Anne produced whisky for both of them and suggested that they should take their drinks out into the garden.

There was a small rectangle of garden behind the little house, in which a mass of roses was in bloom. Canvas chairs had been left out on the lawn, together with some books, a cricket bat, a football and a pile of knitting. Anne curled up in one of the chairs, put her drink down on the grass beside her and picked up the knitting. It looked like a pullover for Martin. She was in a flowery cotton trouser suit, into which she had changed after getting home from work, and her black hair was brushed sleekly back from her face, which was tanned from the weekends that she spent cherishing this patch of suburban garden. She had a narrow oblong of a face, that had a chronic mournfulness about it that gave it a touch of the clown, particularly when it was lit up by her wry, angular smile.

'It's about Hazel,' Richard said after they had sat there peacefully for a minute or two.

'So I supposed.' Anne looked at him with a mixture of gravity and amusement that was characteristic of her. 'Go on,

I'm burning to hear what comes next. Synopsis of story up to this point – hero meets strange woman at party and falls in love with her, but woman has husband who has vanished and whose death she refuses to believe in. Hero tries to make her forget him, but finds himself up against it . . . Second instalment, please go on.'

He laughed. 'I don't think I've ever been cast as a hero before.'

'How do you know?' She smiled at him affectionately. 'Anyway, you *are* in love with her, aren't you?'

'Could be,' he admitted.

'Good old cautious Richard.'

'All right then, I suppose I am. At least I've discovered that I'm viciously jealous of Clyro.'

'Then go ahead and make her forget him.'

'That was my intention. So what does Clyro do? He turns up.'

She let her knitting fall into her lap. 'No!'

'That's what I'm inclined to say myself,' Richard said, 'but Hazel positively thinks yes.'

'I don't understand.'

'It's a rum enough story.'

He went on to tell Anne of his evening with Hazel in the cinema and of what had happened afterwards.

Anne sat listening to him with one hand entangled in the wool of her knitting and the other nursing her glass of whisky, from which she took an occasional sip. When Richard came to the end of his story she stayed silent, thinking it over.

After a little she said, 'Well, it's possible she's right, isn't it?'

'Just,' he agreed.

'But there's something I ought to tell you about Hazel, perhaps,' she said. 'She lives most of the time in some sort of dream. She often isn't in the real world at all.'

'I know that,' he answered.

'Which doesn't mean I'm saying she's a liar, though, as a matter of fact, I think she sometimes is. Not that I really know her very well. Mostly I know her through Jerome and Jeannie, and that really means Jeannie, because she does most of Jerome's thinking for him nowadays. Which is a pity, don't you think, because he's really much the more intelligent of the two.'

'I hardly know Jeannie,' Richard said, 'or Jerome either, if it comes to that. He's changed so much since the old days that he might as well be a stranger.'

'Well, Jeannie's been rich all her life and she's very ambitious and because she's got no special talents of her own all that ambition has to be expressed through Jerome. And that seems to me to have pretty well ruined him, though that isn't how she sees it. Her intentions are excellent. It just happens she loves running other people's lives for them. She'd take mine in hand, if I let her. And trying to sort out Hazel's has become a major project. Jeannie's told me she's sure Hazel's heading for a breakdown, that she has delusions about being followed about London by people who think she can lead them to her husband. Jeannie thinks she ought to be steered to a psychiatrist. And for all I know, she's right. Women like her so often are right, even when they madden you. What do you think yourself? I mean, about this book now.'

'I think Hazel herself is completely convinced Clyro wrote it,' Richard said, 'and the best thing we can do for her is to find out for certain if he did or not.'

'You really are in love with her, aren't you?' Anne said. After a moment she added, 'You know, I'd like to see you go over-board about someone at last, Richard.'

'There's nothing very impressive about going overboard if it's only into shallow water,' he said.

'So for your sake as well as Hazel's we need to find out about Clyro. All right, I'll see what I can do. But don't expect too much. Even in the gossip of the publishing world you come up against the occasional wall of silence. Authors do exist, un-likely as it may seem to you, who simply won't show their faces. And since, if Paul Clyro did write this book, he's certainly acted in a very funny way up to now, he may be funny about that too. But I'll do my best.'

'Thank you.'

'A pleasure.'

They smiled at one another and sipped whisky and went on chatting comfortably among the roses in the gathering dusk.

Two days later Anne telephoned Richard.

Apparently there was no wall of silence surrounding the writer of *Taken As Red*. Without any difficulty at all Anne had discovered that he lived in the village of Vila do Bonfim in Madeira. His novel, which was his first, though he had done a certain amount of freelancing before it, had not made much of a mark in Britain, but had sold very well in America, being serialized there as well as having the film rights sold for a sum rumoured to be about twenty thousand pounds. And because of the success of the film, the British publisher was now re-issuing the book as a paperback, a copy of which Anne had just obtained and posted to Richard.

She added that out of curiosity she had been to see the film the evening before, then had sat up half the night, reading the book, and couldn't help marvelling at the way film companies were ready to pay large sums to authors for books of which they made no real use.

'You'll see, the book and the film are totally different,' she said. 'The film's very tense and straight-faced and exciting, and the book's a mixture of flippancy and romanticism. I suppose the central idea's the same, and they've used the background of the book, and here and there you'll even find patches of the original dialogue. But if the film made Hazel think her husband wrote the book, I think she could easily be wrong. Anyway, you can hand on your copy to her, if she hasn't got hold of one already, and see what she thinks when she's read it. Now this is Gavin Chilmark's address – have you got a pencil? – 7 Rua Ponte Nova, Vila do Bonfim, Madeira . . . Not at all. Delighted. Let me know if there's ever any more detective work you want me to do. It makes a nice change.'

Anne rang off.

Richard turned the situation over in his mind for a moment, then telephoned Hazel.

She was in an unfamiliar state of rage and before he had time to tell her that he had discovered the whereabouts of Gavin Chilmark she told him that she had been to five booksellers that day and not one had had a copy of *Taken As Red* in stock. The book had been published a year ago, and no one, they had all said, could expect them to have it on their shelves.

And when she had ended by ordering a copy she had been told that it might take anything up to three weeks to obtain it from the publisher. She stormed at the inefficiency of the book trade, as if it were all Richard's fault. He said that he was expecting a copy in the next day's post and would bring it round to her in the evening.

'Though I'd really like to read it myself first, if you could bear to wait a day,' he said.

The telephone was silent. Then Hazel said quietly, 'Yes, do that, Richard. Then we can talk about it. It's a good idea.'

'And I've found out where Chilmark lives,' he said.

There was another silence.

At last she said, 'Thank you, Richard. And will you thank Anne for helping.'

'Don't you want the address?' Richard asked.

'Yes, of course. Only . . . well, it can wait till I see you. Till I've read the book, actually. Because, if by any chance I'm wrong . . .'

'I thought you were utterly certain,' Richard said.

'I am.' But she spoke with a new hesitancy. 'All the same, you know how it is. You think about a thing, you live with it, it's always on your mind, and then, all of a sudden, there it is, the thing's happened, and you can't believe it.'

'Perhaps, when it comes to the point, you don't really want to,' he suggested.

'Perhaps,' she said in a subdued voice. 'That would be a funny thing to discover, wouldn't it?'

And a remarkably healthy one, Richard wanted to say, but succeeded in keeping it to himself.

He read the book the following evening. As Anne had said, it was very unlike the film. It was a light, ironic piece of writing about spies in an altogether incredible early-warning station in the Arctic, with slabs of sex inserted into the story at intervals, rather as if the writer had said to himself every so often, 'It's time I sent them to bed again, if the damned thing's going to sell.' The best part of the book, Richard thought, was the background of snow and desolation, of the sense of a small group of people cooped up together in frightening isolation from the rest of the world and beginning to see one another, not as mere human beings, but as monstrous expressions of good and evil.

Uneasily he began to think that this was a book that might have been written by Paul Clyro. Change the snows of the Arctic for those of a winter near Overscaig. Change the early-warning station of the story for the research station where deadly secret work on viruses was being done. Change the characters and their relationships just a little, just enough to be safe from libel, and add the sexual entanglements which sounded unlikely in the Arctic, but which well might have developed in that isolated little community in Sutherland, where the scientists had had their wives living with them, as well as secretaries lodging in the village, and where a little scandal would have helped to pass the long, dark evenings . . .

Practically convinced that Gavin Chilmark and Paul Clyro had been one and the same man, Richard took the book round to Hazel.

She was even quieter than usual that evening, with the air of exhaustion about her of someone who has been working hard to repress an intense excitement.

'Suppose you're right, and I don't say you aren't,' Richard said to her, 'what are you going to do about it?'

They were in her bleak little sitting-room, the sight of which suddenly made Richard furious with Paul Clyro, for having turned Hazel into someone who could care so little about her home, or, for that matter, about anything else. For this was not what she was meant to be, Richard was sure. She was meant to be a woman of strong feelings, a loving woman, passionate and staunch. The waste of it all was an unspeakable crime.

'I haven't decided,' she answered.

'Will you go to Madeira?'

'I haven't decided.'

'But you must have thought about what you'd do if you ever found him.'

'Oh yes, and I've had some ideas about it that would probably shock you. I'm not a nice woman. Far from it.'

'I doubt if we're any of us all that nice.'

'Now I just want to read the book.'

'Yes, of course. But I've had an idea of my own, Hazel.' The idea had come to him only that moment, having been born somehow of her irresolution. 'If you think Chilmark could be your husband, but you aren't certain of it and you want to find out for sure before walking in on him, I might be able to find out for you. I've some time off due to me and I've no objection to spending it in Madeira. Quite a nice thing to do, actually.'

She sat there as if she had not heard him. She was holding the paperback in both hands and was looking vaguely in front of her at some point a little above Richard's head.

'It's only a suggestion,' he said after a pause, feeling that undoubtedly he had blundered.

'Yes, and . . . Yes, it's a wonderful suggestion.' Her voice was still quiet and dead. 'Then I wouldn't have to risk arriving on the doorstep of a total stranger and saying "I'm so sorry, I thought I was your wife." It's a wonderful suggestion, Richard. Thank you so much.'

'Then you mean you'd like me to do it.' For some reason he was taken by surprise, and he began to wonder how seriously he had meant his offer.

'Oh, I don't know – not yet,' she said. 'But it's so good of you to think of it. It's like you. You know, you're a much nicer person than Paul. I wish I'd met you before I met him. So much might have been different.'

'It could be different still, couldn't it?'

Her gaze came back from far away to meet his.

'Richard, I'm *scared* – that's what's wrong with me just now. So don't expect too much sense out of me. I'm scared this writer could turn out to be Paul and that I'd have to face what you said the other evening, that he walked out on me cold-bloodedly and deliberately and has been getting along quite happily and successfully without me. And I'm equally scared that this man is just a genuine Gavin Chilmark, whom I've never met in my life, and that my poor Paul is dead, or lost and mad, and that I'm never going to find out the truth about him. I'm scared of everything.'

'Who wouldn't be? You don't have to explain it. But if you want me to go to Madeira, I'm willing.'

Leaving her still clutching the paperback with both hands, he let himself out of the flat.

The next day he had a visit in his office from Jeannie Otter-shaw.

It was in the afternoon, and he had just been dealing with an old customer, whom he knew well, who had come in to buy the Clarendon Press collection of the letters of Horace Walpole, which had been in the window of the Farcet Street shop, and had gone out with the Nonesuch Press edition of the Bible instead. Jeannie was in a silk suit of shocking pink, with black gloves and a black velvet bow in her glistening grey hair, and was also in a furious temper.

'You may be busy, but you've got to find time to see me,' she said with a rasp in the deep voice that issued so surprisingly from her thin little throat and bird-like body. She dropped abruptly into a chair facing Richard across his desk. 'Jerome and I expected you to *help* us with Hazel, not to drive her completely over the edge. What's this about the two of you going off on a wild goose chase to find Paul Clyro in Madeira?'

'Is that what Hazel told you we were going to do?' Richard asked.

'Well isn't it?' Jeannie said. 'Honestly, Richard, I thought you had more sense and decency. You simply must not do this. *You must not!* Do you understand? Take her to Italy, to Greece, to Blackpool, any damned where and good luck to you both – it would be very good for her. But to take Hazel off somewhere, in the state she's in, on the vague promise that she might find Paul there – it would be wicked. I'm not being prudish, I think an honest-to-goodness love-affair would be the best thing that could happen to Hazel, but to lead her along with promises of finding that insufferable Paul . . . I can't, I simply can't find words to tell you what I think of it.'

'I don't suppose I could either, if you'd got the story right.' Richard had reacted as he often did to the anger of others by becoming abnormally calm. 'But why, if you don't mind my asking, do you speak of "that insufferable Paul"? I thought he was rather a friend of yours and Jerome's.'

'*Was, was!*' she stormed at him. 'A long time ago. Before he treated Hazel as he did. Not that I ever cared for him much. But he was one of Jerome's closer friends, so I did my best to put up with him. I always try to endure Jerome's friends, and I can tell you, it isn't always easy. He's got so many, for one thing, and he's got no discrimination. It's that bloody golden heart of his that makes him collect some of the weirdest people.'

'What was wrong with Paul Clyro?' Richard asked. 'I mean, apart from his disappearing.'

'Oh, nothing much. He was just wholly insignificant, that's all, a born AEIOU.'

'A what?'

She gave her deep laugh. 'You don't live in a world of initials, do you? Jerome and I do. For instance, Jerome's a DSA in the CPS. And the man who's one grade higher is an SDSA. And there are people, like that man Wolsingham, who killed himself, if you know who I'm talking about, who are SSSAs. And you can describe almost everyone else we know by a string of initials. So I've made up a string or two of my own, and AEIOU is one of them.'

'What does it stand for?'

'Assistant Experimental Inferior Official Underdog.'

'And that's what Paul Clyro was like?'

'Actually, I created the grade just for him,' she said. 'It's what he was. A born underling. And that's a way of saying a bit of a parasite too, because he couldn't survive without a Wolsingham to inject some spirit into him.'

'You seem to have a rather high opinion of Wolsingham.'

'Oh, I only met him a few times. But he was a fantastically attractive man. Absolutely unbelievable.'

'That isn't how your husband described him to me.'

'No, of course not. I'm giving you a woman's viewpoint. Mind you, I'm not saying I liked him, or that I trusted him an inch, but he had a quite fabulous charm.'

'Most people seem to have trusted him pretty far, however, including the Clyros.'

'They were both such innocent young things,' she said. 'But you've made me wander from the point. What I came to say was that to get Hazel to go off to Madeira with you on a crazy chase after Paul would be wicked. It would probably completely destroy her mentally. I mean to do my utmost to stop it.'

'There's no need for you to trouble.' It amused Richard to

find Jeannie reminding him of Harriet. There was no trace of outward similarity between them, but both had minds that dealt in simple certainties about other people's business. But Harriet was a placid woman, without the nervous temper that seethed in Jeannie. If you disagreed with Harriet, she pitied you for being so stupid and easily forgave you. Jeannie, he thought, would do neither. 'There was never any question of our going to Madeira together. I merely suggested that as I'd a holiday due to me I might spend it in Madeira, and while I was there see what I could find out about this man Gavin Chilmark.'

'That's all?' Jeannie gave him a long, probing look.

'That's absolutely all.'

Impulsively she held out a hand to him.

'I'm a fool,' she said. 'I ought to have listened to Jerome. He said you'd never do anything so foolish as to take her looking for Paul. He said you were much too level-headed. Will you forgive me?'

'But has Hazel really told you she's going to Madeira?' Richard asked.

'I think at least she's considering it,' Jeannie answered.

'Then she's read the book and made up her mind that Clyro wrote it.'

'Oh yes, she's got no doubt of that whatever.'

'And what do you think she'll do when she finds him?'

Jeannie stood up. 'Your guess is as good as mine. She's very unpredictable, as you probably know by now. And some of what happened would depend on Paul, wouldn't it? On what he did about her suddenly turning up. If he's stayed away all this time of his own accord, it isn't likely he's going to welcome her, is it? You know, I've often wondered if there wasn't more the matter with that marriage all along than Hazel's ever admitted. She's terribly proud. I think if Paul really left her for another woman, say, she might try not to let anyone know – perhaps not even to admit it to herself. I know Jerome's always believed they were utterly devoted to one another, but I've never been so sure. But if you go to Madeira, Richard, how will you know if the man is Paul or not? You've never met him.'

'I can ask him,' Richard said.

'And if he simply says he isn't?'

'I suppose there's some photograph I can take with me.'

'Well, I rather hope now you'll go and find out the truth,' she said. 'But don't let Hazel go.'

'I don't think I've actually much influence over her,' he said.

She laughed. 'I don't think anybody has. I don't think anybody ever has had. She's always gone her own way, not making a fuss about it, but never taking much notice of anybody else. Goodbye, and I'm sorry I came rushing in here in that fool fashion.'

She left, with Richard seeing her down the stairs to the street then returning in a very thoughtful mood to his office. That evening he told Hazel of Jeannie's visit.

Hazel said contemptuously. 'She's so stupid. All theories and no brains of her own. To jump to a conclusion like that . . . ! I often have to remind myself rather carefully that she means well.' Pausing, she added uncertainly, 'But perhaps I did talk a bit incoherently. I'd just read the book and I was absolutely certain that only Paul could have written it, and I felt I had to talk to someone, so I rang her up, and I suppose I talked pretty wildly.'

'Are you still as certain now that Clyro wrote it?' Richard asked.

'Oh, yes. I've actually gone back and checked certain passages, and I *know* Paul wrote it. But I've had time to calm down and think, and I realize it would be asking too much of you to send you off to see him. So please don't worry about it. Forget you ever suggested it.'

'Which were the parts of the book that made you so sure that Clyro wrote it?' Richard wanted to know.

'What would you expect?' She gave a bitter little smile. 'One or two of the love-scenes. I happen to remember them rather well. And there they are – the naked truth about them. I'm afraid I cried when I read them.'

'All right, I'll go,' Richard said.

'But I'm not asking you to – really I'm not.' She sounded genuinely reluctant.

58

'I'll need a photograph, of course,' he said, 'in case he simply says he's Gavin Chilmark and that's that.'

'But truly, Richard . . . ' She broke off with a faint shrug. Getting up, she fumbled about in one of the drawers, pulling out odd papers and notebooks, then extracted a passport. She opened it and took a thoughtful look at it.

'It's shockingly bad of him, but it's all I've got,' she said.

Richard took the passport. The face in the picture stared at him with the touch of menace that somehow appears in nearly all passport photographs. To judge by them, it could easily be supposed that the people who go travelling are mainly a gang of dangerous schizophrenics.

'It's out of date,' he said.

'Yes,' she agreed.

'Didn't he have a more recent one?'

'Not that I know of.'

'It wasn't out of date when he left.'

'No.'

'Yet he didn't take it with him.'

'I've told you, he didn't take anything.'

'Then how did he get out of the country to Madeira?'

'I suppose he could have got hold of a forged one, couldn't he?'

'Would he have known how to set about doing that? If I wanted to do it myself, I shouldn't even know where to start.'

'How do I know what he'd know?' Her voice shot up in the way it sometimes did when she was excited. 'Don't you realize that the one thing I know about him is that I never knew anything about him at all?'

Richard nodded. 'How long ago was this photograph taken?'

'How long has it been out of date? About a year, isn't it? And they last for five years without having to be renewed. So that makes it six years. I remember we got the passports for a holiday in Italy, then we went to Norway the year after, and couldn't afford to go anywhere the year after that, so those two times are the only times we used them.'

'In six years he may have altered a good deal.'

'Perhaps.'

The photograph showed a longish face with a pointed chin

with a deep cleft in it, a high, narrow forehead with thick, light-coloured hair standing up from it, a straight mouth and eyes that stared straight and hard at the camera. The description in the passport said that Paul Clyro was six foot one, had light brown hair, grey eyes and no distinguishing marks.

'Well, it's better than nothing,' Richard said and pocketed the passport.

Only after he had done so, he realized that at that moment, with that action, he had committed himself to going to Madeira to look for Paul Clyro.

Chapter Five

Next day Richard went to a travel agent and bought a ticket to Funchal on the coming Friday.

The plane left Heathrow in the early afternoon. He had to change at Lisbon and after that it was a little over an hour to Madeira. The whole journey took less than six hours.

It was intensely hot in the airport at Lisbon. After it, the comfortable air-conditioned coolness of the plane to Funchal made Richard drowsy and soon after it had taken off he fell into a doze. He woke to think that he was looking at Madeira. There was a small black island out there, rising craggily out of thick white stationary billows. Still half-asleep, he thought how strange it was that Madeira should be so small and that the sea should have that curious white foggy texture. Then he realized that what he was looking at were mountain peaks, projecting through masses of dense cloud.

The plane began to circle. Sometimes the peaks were on the left and sometimes on the right, and a faint sense of tension began to build up among the passengers as they wondered how long it would be before the pilot decided that he could take them down through the cloud-cover, or must take them back to Lisbon. It was during this time that a bald-headed man in a seat three rows ahead of Richard turned and looked directly at him.

He did it suddenly, in the way that a person sometimes seems to do if he feels that he is being stared at from behind. For a moment their eyes met. The man's eyes were almost lashless and he had only the faintest of eyebrows, so that his whole face looked bald. It was smooth, pale, and slightly shiny. He gave Richard a puzzled look, as if he wondered where he had seen him before, then turned away again.

A moment later thick mist swam against the windows of the plane, there was the sensation of dropping sharply, and suddenly they were under the clouds, with the fertile slopes of the island looking startlingly close to them. Then they were taxiing up the narrow runway of the little airport between the hills and the sea.

Richard allowed one of the hotel touts outside the airport building to annex him, place him in a taxi and send him off along a road that wound around the base of the hills towards Funchal.

It seemed a long way, and Richard was tired. The taxi, in a long stream of others, swept through two or three villages with narrow streets, whitewashed, red-roofed churches, and always the calm expanse of the Atlantic, a soft blue under the roof of cloud, on their left hand. Funchal itself seemed to be a roaring chaos of taxis. Richard had never before seen so many gathered in one place, waiting in long ranks or curvetting wildly in the streets, blaring their horns at one another. How, he wondered, could the drivers, with so much competition, make a living? His own driver talked incessantly, pointing out the cathedral, the harbour, the Botanic Gardens, and naming every plant that they passed, the jacarandas, the allamandas, the frangipanes, which he had somehow learnt were likely to be unfamiliar to a visitor from a northern country. He spoke astonishingly good English. While he was talking, it occurred to Richard that this man had probably never felt cold in his life. Wasn't the climate of Madeira more or less the same the whole year round? Richard tried to imagine what it would be like never to experience anything chillier than this evening, never to huddle in heavy clothes against the bitterness of the winter, never to feel surprised gratitude for a half day of sunshine and warmth. Oddly, he was not sure that he would enjoy it. Some degree of discomfort in life seemed so normal that he thought that he might easily lose all sense of balance, of security, without it. However, he was disappointed in the clouds that hid the sky which here, he felt, should have been of unbroken blue.

He asked the driver if they had much of this weather.

'Sometimes, sometimes,' the man said, 'at this time of year. But in the morning is fine, you will see.'

And in the morning it was indeed fine.

Richard's bedroom, in the hotel to which the taxi delivered him, had a balcony facing the sea and when his breakfast was brought to him he had the tray set down on the table out of doors. But in a few minutes the burning heat of the sun had driven him back into his room, taking his tray with him, the butter on it already reduced to a little yellow puddle.

It was necessary now to think about Gavin Chilmark and how to approach him. The evening before Richard had put him out of his mind. He had had a couple of drinks in the bar, dinner in a big dining-room, then had gone to bed early. He had, however, studied a map of the island which was on the wall of the bar. The village of Vila do Bonfim was on the coast to the west of Funchal. The distance to it was not very great, so a taxi seemed the obvious means of transport. A taxi with another English-speaking driver. And a good time to arrive at Gavin Chilmark's home might be the later part of the morning. So there was time for a swim first. Richard put on his swimming trunks and made his way down to the swimming pool.

Lying in the sun, after a swim, with other inert bodies stretched out around him, tanned, or scarlet and peeling, or as pale as his own, he tried to work out what he was going to say to the man whom he was going to visit. It might have been sensible to think about this sooner. But Richard had the feeling that for the last few days he had been swept along by a current too powerful for him to do more, while he was in its grip, than just keep his head above water.

His own actions, now that he was lying here, sun-drenched and refreshed, considerably astonished him. And where had they landed him?

On a lovely island, with palm trees, hibiscus and plumbago

all around him, and wishing that he had no need to do anything but go on lying where he was, drowsing and dreaming. That was really all that he felt like doing just then. Hazel and her problems had become curiously remote, while the picture of her that came to his mind seemed wraithlike and pallid compared with the bare brown bodies around him.

At the far end of the pool a girl dived off the diving board into the blue water. She came up with her blonde hair clinging wetly round her face. Or so Richard thought until he realized, from the way that she tossed it back, that the wet hair was a wig. Flowing false hair, which was a bathing cap which covered dry hair. Could anything be more fantastic? Layer on layer of reality. Or of falsification, whichever way you preferred to look at it. It made him ponder on whether Gavin Chilmark would turn out to be a real Gavin Chilmark, or a false one, only wearing that identity to save Paul Clyro's from getting wet, from going under in an unsympathetic world and drowning.

But Richard knew that he must soon nerve himself to call on this perfect stranger and say to him, 'If you're who I think you may be, I'm here to tell you I mean to persuade your wife to divorce you, because I want to marry her myself. And it will make everything so much easier for everybody if you'll co-operate by at least admitting who you are . . . '

Or words to that effect.

And if the stranger should simply say, 'I don't know what you're talking about . . . '

What then?

There was the passport photograph, of course, but it was old. It might be useless.

Richard gave an inward groan and stood up. If he did not get on with the job, he would soon be finding good reasons for putting it off until tomorrow. And if tomorrow, why not the day after? Draping his shirt round his faintly tingling shoulders, he returned to his room, dressed and went to the hall porter to ask him to find him a taxi.

The porter sent a boy out to whistle for one of the black Mercedes diesels that waited in a long rank near the hotel. The car felt hot as an oven from waiting in the sun. The road to Vila do Bonfim wound between banana plantations and vine-yards, with gay clumps of agapanthus and geraniums growing along the verges. Every inch of the good red soil seemed to be cultivated. The steep hillsides were terraced to their summits, and covered in lush green. Even a good many of the houses were almost hidden under a load of vines trained over their roofs. The road climbed steeply, descended and climbed again, some-times veering into the hills to edge around some inlet of the sea, sometimes following the line of the dark cliffs, high above it.

Vila do Bonfim was built around a small square that over-looked a harbour. There was a small, gaily painted bandstand in the middle of the square, and a white-walled, red-roofed church along one side of it. The square was empty except for three or four men lounging in the shade of some golden blossomed acacias. The taxi stopped near them and the driver called something out to them. Richard guessed that he was asking them where to find Rua Ponte Nova. But before the men had time to answer, hordes of children appeared from nowhere, converging on the car, every one with an eager little hand held out and drowning the replies of the man by their shrill voices piping hungrily, 'Escudo! Escudo!'

The first thing that Richard noticed about the children was their beauty, the fine features of their delicate, dark faces, their radiantly beguiling smiles, the grace of their slim, lively bodies. But when the driver drove on, the faces in an instant were all twisted into grimaces of anger. The children shouted after the car words that it was easy to guess were obscenities, and one or two threw pebbles after it that rattled against the windows.

The driver seemed unconcerned. But to Richard the sudden hostility of it was startling and shocking. Not one of the children could have been over ten, yet all at once they had shown the ferocity of a rioting mob. Richard recoiled from them all the more sharply because at first he had been charmed. He almost failed, during the next few minutes, to notice the extraordinary beauty of the village.

Its harbour was formed by a jagged arm of black volcanic rock that curved out as if to embrace the shoulder of the cliff on the far side of a small lagoon, as blue as lapis lazuli in its strange dark setting. The beach, where a number of fishing-boats, most of them painted a light blue, had been drawn up, was of great flat black pebbles. Brightly coloured washing had been spread out on the pebbles to dry. The cottages above the harbour were white or cream-coloured, with red pantile roofs that curved up orientally at the corners, with little figures, doves, or angels, or small gargoyles at the points of the eaves. Everywhere the colours were sharp, clear and clean under the strong wash of the morning sunlight.

7 Rua Ponte Nova was a little white house halfway up the hill behind the village. The house seemed to crouch against the hillside, as if it had been built right into it. Richard paid off the taxi and walked up to the door. When he was close to it he saw that the paint on it was chipped and blistered. Also the plaster on the walls was cracked and in places flaking away. But the small, steeply sloping garden was well kept, with a fig tree in it, roses, marigolds and flame-red alstroemerias. There was a datura near the door, a big bush covered in hanging trumpets of blossom, apricot coloured. Their scent was almost too strong and too sweet. From the corners of the curved eaves of the red pantile roof little winged cherubs smiled down at him.

The door was ajar.

As Richard put out a hand to knock on it, he heard a woman's voice inside, singing in English. The song was a pop song that he vaguely recognized about the agonies of not being loved enough. The singer's voice was soft and contented. When Richard knocked the sound stopped abruptly and something was called out to him in Portuguese.

He cleared his throat apologetically and said, 'Good morning. I was looking for Mr Chilmark.'

There was a brief silence, then footsteps crossed the floor inside and the door was opened.

Richard thought that she was about seventeen. After a few minutes he was to revise his estimate. She was perhaps as much as twenty-two or twenty-three. But there was a faint chubbiness about her which gave her a look of adolescence. Her cheeks were soft and full, her chin was rounded, her nose was small and turned slightly upward, and her eyes were blue, big, a little surprised, but friendly. Her straight fair hair was parted in the middle and hung loose down her back. She was wearing a very short cotton dress, much washed, with sandals. Her arms and legs, sun-toasted to a mellow brown, were beautiful.

'I'm so sorry, he's gone out,' she said. 'But come in, won't you? I don't think he'll be long. I'm Gillian Chilmark.' She appeared to have no fear of letting a stranger into the house when she was alone. 'The place is a mess, I'm afraid. I wasn't expecting a visitor. Not that it isn't always a mess. Gavin sometimes goes round tidying up, but he says I'm hopeless. And specially at the moment, because I'm dressmaking. You can't dressmake and keep a room tidy, can you? Have you ever known anyone who could? It isn't reasonable to expect it.'

It was not a matter to which Richard had ever given any thought, but he saw what she meant. The small and rather dark whitewashed room was furnished with basket chairs with bright cushions on them, on each of which, it seemed to him as he glanced around, there were pieces of material, or of paper patterns, or scissors, boxes of pins or reels of thread. A tape-measure trailed across the floor. In the middle of the room stood an ironing-board with an iron on it, with the flex of the iron attached to the central light above. A plain wooden table under the window had an old-fashioned and very battered-looking sewing-machine on it, with some pieces of material lying beside it. There was a singey smell in the room.

'Forgive me for asking, but is that iron turned off?' Richard asked.

She gave a squeak and cried, 'Oh God, no! Thank you for reminding me.' She lunged at the switch, then swept some of the clutter off a chair and said, 'Do sit down. Would you like a drink? There's some Madeira and some wine – Choupal, I think – do you know they call it black wine here? I mean, what we call red wine they call black wine. Doesn't it sound sinister? Or, of course, there's coffee. Instant. I'm no good at making the real kind. For that you'd have to wait till Gavin gets here. Are you a friend of his?'

But the last question, Richard thought, was only thrown in as a kind of politeness. He would have received as warm a welcome if he had walked in from outer space.

He said that he would enjoy a cup of coffee.

She answered, 'Coming up,' and disappeared into the kitchen. He heard her there filling a kettle and banging on its lid.

When she reappeared, he said, 'Actually I've never met Mr Chilmark, but I very much want to talk to him.'

It was untrue. At that moment he did not want to talk to Gavin Chilmark at all. A Mrs Chilmark, particularly one as young and friendly as this one, was something for which he had not allowed.

'Is it about the book, or the film, or something?' she asked. 'He never remembers to tell me.'

'It's about a – personal matter,' Richard said.

'Money!' She sat down at the table, picking up a half-smoked cigarette and attaching it to her full, soft, lower lip. 'A personal matter – that's what people always say when it's money and they want to be tactful, because they think I don't look old enough to know about it. But I know much more than Gavin. I'm very businesslike about it. And anyway, we've got lots of money now, so don't worry, we'll be able to straighten everything out . . . Oh, look at me, not offering you a cigarette! Do you smoke?' She held out a half-empty packet to him and when he shook his head, went straight on, 'Gavin's given it up, think of that! Such strength of will. Most of the time he lets you think he hasn't a will of his own at all, and then he does something dramatic like that. But he waited until we got rich to do it, isn't that maddening? When we were poor, getting fish cheap off some of the fishermen he knows and eating an awful sort of brown cheese and drinking wine only about once a week, I used to beg him to stop smoking, just to save the money, and he wouldn't listen to me. He'd say, "Don't bother me, I have to have some vices, don't I?" Well, I never could understand that. Don't you think it was an odd thing to say? I mean, why does a person have to have vices? Have you any? Do you feel you simply couldn't get on without them?'

'I suppose I do rather cherish those I've got,' Richard said. 'But isn't that noise your kettle boiling?'

'Oh God, so it is!' She leapt towards the kitchen door.

In a minute or two she returned with two cups of coffee and a sugar-bowl on a tray. Some of the coffee had slopped into each saucer.

'I'm awfully sorry, I put milk in them both, without thinking,' she said. 'Would you prefer it black? I'll make some more if you would. It's powdered milk, of course. Do you know, we can't get fresh milk here? It all gets made into butter and cheese and sent to Portugal. Probably you don't think we've even got any cows. You may not have seen any. They're all kept in those little thatched houses you see everywhere that look like privies, near the cottages, and the cows never get out, poor dears, except when someone takes them for a walk, which I expect you think is dreadfully cruel, but you see, the slopes are so steep that you couldn't let them just wander around, they'd break their poor legs. You haven't been here long, have you?'

'I only got here yesterday evening,' Richard said.

'It's your colour, you see. That's how I guessed. You're still pale pink.'

'Have you been here long?'

'About two years. I came for a holiday with my aunts and met Gavin and never went away.'

'You seem to speak Portuguese very fluently.'

'Oh, I'm good at languages,' she said without arrogance. 'I speak French and German and a bit of Russian too. I'm not very good at Russian. I've never been there, you see, it's all out of books. But if I'm in a place for only a few months, as I was in France and Germany, I find I can soon get around pretty well. I had a wonderful education. It's one of the things my aunts believed in. Education, they said, that's what counts. Nowadays class distinctions are getting all muddled up, but with education you can make it. So they sent me to a fantastically expensive boarding-school, and then to France, and then to Germany, and then they took me on the wonderful cruise that brought me here. And about our second day here Gavin picked me up and I decided to become a drop-out with him. Sometimes I feel bad about it, my poor, mad, darling aunts were so disappointed. Of course . . . ' She paused and smiled charmingly. 'I'm not really married to Gavin. You guessed that, didn't you? People always do, for some reason.'

'Perhaps because you tell them,' Richard suggested.

She considered it. 'But I feel them guessing it, you see, so I think I may as well tell them as have them think me a hypocrite. He's got a wife somewhere or other, he says.' She had picked up some of her sewing and was pulling out tacking-threads.

Richard drank some of his coffee.

'Aren't you sure?'

'Yes, I'm sure – except that she might be dead. He never hears from her.'

'He hasn't divorced her?'

'No, he just walked out. But only after she'd done the most frightful things to him.'

'Such as?'

'Oh, she just made him utterly miserable. She simply drove him to leave her.' She had begun sticking pins into her sewing and had several in her mouth. 'That personal matter you want to talk to Gavin about,' she said through them, 'if it isn't about money, it's about Margaret, isn't it? Do you want him to divorce her? Do you want to marry her yourself?'

Her intuitiveness bothered him.

'Margaret?' he said.

'Well, that's her name, isn't it?'

'If it is, then I've come to the wrong place and I'd better go away and leave you in peace.' He added, 'I think that cigarette of yours is just about to start burning a hole in the table.'

She had put the cigarette down on the edge of an ashtray when she had picked up her sewing, where the stub had been smouldering away until this moment, when it had just fallen, unnoticed by her, on the table. There were a good many burns there already.

'Oh God, so it is!' She snatched up the stub and pounded it out in the ashtray. 'Thank you for telling me. And please don't go away. Wait till Gavin gets here. He loves having people to talk to. So do I. Let me warn you, though, if you do want to marry Margaret, she made his life a hell. Not that I ought to say a thing like that, ought I? If you're in love with her, I mean, you'll hate me for it. And I'm naturally biased. She may be very nice, for all I know, but just not suited to Gavin. That can happen, you know.'

'So I've been told,' Richard said.

'I mean, two perfectly delightful people can simply hate each other. It makes it very difficult for anyone who happens to like them both. You're sure to like Gavin . . . Oh, here he is now.' There had been the sound of a car in the road, which she had apparently recognized. 'Good – you can sort out with him whether or not you ought to marry Margaret. And if you want him to divorce her, I'm sure he will, he's awfully good-natured. Gavin – ' She raised her voice. 'We've got a visitor.'

Footsteps came up the short path to the door and as Richard got to his feet a man came into the room.

The newcomer was about six foot one, as Paul Clyro was stated to be in the passport that Richard had in his pocket. He had light brown hair and grey eyes. But the passport claimed that he had no distinguishing marks, and this man had several. For one, he had a strong, curly beard that covered most of his face, and though the hair on the top of his head was an indeterminate brown, the beard was reddish. Also, one of his grey eyes was noticably larger than the other, and the blinking of the two did not synchronize. As he stood in the doorway, taking his first look at Richard, he seemed to be giving him a knowing wink. At the same time, one corner of Chilmark's mouth went up in a crooked twitch of a smile. Yet in spite of his tic, this man looked expansive, good-humoured and self-confident. He was wearing jeans, a loose shirt and sandals, and was carrying a basket which contained a loaf of bread and a variety of vegetables, courgettes, peppers, aubergines, gem-like in their rich, polished colours.

Later Richard was to try to remember just what his first impression of Gavin Chilmark had been.

Had it been that this man was almost certainly Paul Clyro, or that he was not?

Had Richard actually felt anything except confusion?

Chapter Six

The girl said, 'Gavin, this is . . . ' She paused and looked at Richard. 'You never told me your name.'

'I don't suppose she gave you time to tell her,' Chilmark said with the odd smile that made his whole face look crooked.

Richard realized that at some time in his life this man had probably had a disease called Bell's palsy, which can leave one side of the face with a permanent slight paralysis. A perfect disguise supplied to him by nature if in fact it had happened only recently.

'My name's Richard Hedon,' he said.

'And he wants to marry Margaret, so you'll have to pull yourself together and divorce her,' the girl said.

'Is that true?' Gavin Chilmark asked.

'Up to a point,' Richard answered, 'but Mrs Chilmark is going rather fast for me.'

'You don't have to call me Mrs Chilmark,' she said. 'It only makes me self-conscious. I'm Gillian.'

'Let's have a drink on it, anyway,' Chilmark said. 'Any friend of Margaret's is a friend of mine – if she has any friends. She used never to go in for them much. Not what I personally call friends, the word being one to which I attach some importance. Let's have a drink. Gillian, let's have some of that Choupal.'

'Black wine!' she hissed at him. 'I don't think it sounds lucky to baptize a new friendship in black wine.'

'Look, in any other country you'd call it red wine and be perfectly happy about it,' Chilmark said. 'Besides, who said anything about friendship? Didn't I explain it's a word I speak with care? But why not let's help a new acquaintance get off to a good start?'

Gillian put down her sewing and disappeared into the kitchen again.

Chilmark went on, 'I've just been down to the shops. I do most of our marketing to try to work up my Portuguese. Gillian doesn't need to. Foreign languages just come dripping off her tongue. She's a very intelligent girl, by the way, in case you hadn't noticed. She doesn't always want people to notice. Anyway, the shops fascinate me. They're dark little caverns with their ceilings all hung with vegetables and bunches of herbs and sausages and shoes and hats and holy pictures and – would you believe it? – plastic flowers. Here, in a place where you can get almost any flower on earth to grow, you can still buy plastic flowers. Is there any limit to the strangeness of the human mind?'

He had dropped into one of the basket chairs and was lolling there with his knees apart and his hands hanging down between them.

Richard said abruptly, 'What I'm really here for is to ask you, are you Paul Clyro?'

The other man raised his eyebrows. One eyebrow went up much farther than the other. 'Am I *who*?'

'Paul Clyro.'

'That's an odd name.'

'Yes.'

'And it's a bit of an odd question you're asking.'

'It can't seem so odd if you *are* Paul Clyro.'

'Only I'm not.' Chilmark's winking gaze on Richard had become extremely thoughtful. 'How's that? Does it get us any farther?'

'I'm not sure if it does or not.'

'May I ask you what's given you the idea that I might be this man, whoever he is?'

Richard took his wallet out of his pocket, extracted Paul Clyro's old passport and handed it to the man in the chair.

As he was looking at it, the girl came back into the room with a tray, glasses and a bottle of wine. Putting them down, she looked over Chilmark's shoulder at the photograph.

'Who's that?' she asked.

'Mr Hedon thinks it's me,' Chilmark said.

'Seriously?'

'I think he's serious.'

'You aren't nearly as good-looking as that.'

'That's one of the things I was thinking.' He handed the passport back to Richard. His manner was relaxed and friendly. 'Suppose you tell me the rest of the story.'

Richard looked deeply into the glass that the girl poured out for him. The wine in it was red, but as he gazed into it it seemed to grow darker, to turn opaque and black.

'It's complicated,' he said.

'I like stories complicated, though I don't write them that, way. You can't make a good film out of anything too involved.'

'Well, once upon a time there was a man called Paul Clyro,', Richard said. 'I never met him. I know very little about him. He became a scientist. I believe a molecular biologist. And he married a girl called Hazel.'

'Ah,' Chilmark said, 'enter the love interest.'

'But there's another love interest in the story,' Richard said. 'A quite different kind of love interest. Clyro's hero-worship of the man he was working with. A man called Wolsingham.'

'That name rings a bell.'

'It should. Wolsingham was head of a research station near Overscaig in Sutherland, where they were doing something very secret about viruses, the results of which he kept handing on, over the years, to the Russians. But the security people were closing in on him, and he knew it, and one day he took his own life in his laboratory by swallowing potassium cyanide. All that got into the newspapers.'

Was it imagination that the face of the man before him had grown a little tauter than before? With the growth of beard on it and the way that the one eye winked, it was hard to be sure.

'Yes, I remember it,' Chilmark said.

'And Paul Clyro found the body,' Richard went on. 'It must have been a fearful shock. Not just the shock of walking in on a corpse, but of discovering the kind of man he'd venerated, and being questioned and investigated and suspected himself. So it would seem he was driven half mad, because one day he walked out of his home, leaving his wife expecting him home for lunch, and he's never been seen from that day to this.'

The man and the girl were both listening to him with deep interest. As Richard paused Gillian leaned forward and tapped him on the knee with a finger that had a thimble on it.

'I do like you,' she said. 'I like you enormously. We've never had anyone else come in here and tell us anything like this. What happened next?'

73

Chilmark reached for her hand and kept possession of it.

'Don't confuse him,' he said. 'The story's coming along very nicely. Mr Hedon must have done a great deal of thinking about it to be able to tell it so lucidly.' He drank some wine. 'Well?' he said.

'There isn't much more to tell,' Richard replied, 'except to say that I met Hazel Clyro some weeks ago, and if that isn't very long, I know her well enough to see that's she's never got over what happened to her. She's unhappy, she's lonely, she's shut herself off from people, she's not very stable. And every day of her life, I believe, she's half-convinced Clyro will walk in at her door.'

'So you yourself haven't been able to get very far with her,' Chilmark said. 'But what put you on to the idea that I might be Clyro?'

'It was Hazel herself and that book you wrote,' Richard said. 'Hazel says she and her husband plotted a book together which was to be called *Taken As Red*, and apparently, when it was published in England, she didn't see it around –'

'It was a flop there,' Chilmark interrupted. 'But it did well in America, and nicely in translations too even before I sold the film rights.'

'The first time she said anything about it,' Richard said, 'was when she and I went to the cinema to see the film *Pardon Me For Dying*. That's when she saw the name of the book the film had been adapted from. She nearly collapsed. She said the writer couldn't be anyone but her husband. And afterwards, when she got hold of the book, she said several of the scenes in it were straight descriptions of things that had happened between them. The effect on her was shattering. So I decided the only thing for me to do was to find out where you lived and to come and see you and try to find out if there was any substance to her belief or not. So that's what I've done. And either she's right, or else I've committed such an impertinence that probably – that's my impression of you – you'll easily forgive me for it.'

They were both looking at him gravely. Their expressions were interested and sympathetic, not antagonistic, not apprehensive, not amused. Richard had the feeling that if only the circumstances had been different, here were two people with whom he would very quickly have made friends.

'Do you know, I half-wish Gavin *was* this Paul Clyro of yours,' Gillian said. 'Then she could divorce him, and you could marry her, and your "once upon a time" could end "and they lived happily ever after".'

Chilmark nodded. 'Yes. The problem is, however, how do I go about proving I'm not this man?'

'You could put Mr Hedon in touch with some of your old friends in England,' Gillian said.

Chilmark appeared to meet this suggestion without enthusiasm. He did not answer.

She went on, 'Or you could go to London and meet Mrs Clyro and let her see you're not her husband.'

'Yes, I could do that,' Chilmark said. 'Only I'm damned if I want to go to London or anywhere else just at the moment, simply because a complete stranger walks in on me and tells me he thinks I may be someone I'm not. Forgive me,' he added to Richard, 'but although I sympathize with your difficulties, it's asking rather a lot. I've just got another book started. It's coming along rather well. I don't want any serious interruptions.'

'Then why shouldn't she come here?' Gillian asked. 'Suppose I write to her and ask her to come and stay with us. Would she come, Richard, or is she too grand for us? Our spare room is just an awful little attic. But after all, this *is* Madeira, so she might like to come here just for the sunshine and everything, even if Gavin isn't her husband. And he's a super cook. You could promise her good food. He'd love to have her, you know. I keep asking our friends to come and stay with us. It isn't that we're lonely, but I do love old faces. But so often the poor darlings can't afford the journey, any more than we would have been able to in the old days. Do you think she could?'

'And just what should we do,' Chilmark asked with his tight, lop-sided grin, 'if she arrived, and threw her arms about me, and declared I was her husband, and please could she have a share of all my recent profits? Not a divorce – no, no. Just a fair share.'

'Oh God!' Gillian exclaimed, looking at him in dismay. 'I hadn't thought of that. What on earth *would* we do?'

'Put it out of your minds!' Richard retorted harshly. 'That's something you can do at once.'

There was a slight pause, then Chilmark said, 'I'm sorry – I'm sure we can.' He returned the passport to Richard. 'My remark was ill-judged. But writing the kind of thing I'm trying to write at the moment somehow develops the suspicious side of one's nature. One has to learn to take note of all the dreadful possibilities implicit in any situation. Your friend Hazel Clyro may be labouring under an absolutely genuine and very tragic delusion, or she may, she just may, have thought out a rather smart racket.'

'Or she may, she just may,' Richard said, 'be right.'

For what had that face been like before the reddish beard had covered it? What was the chin like under the beard? Was it long and narrow, with a cleft in it? What had Chilmark's gaze been like before illness had partly paralyzed one of the eyelids? What had his body been like before time had thickened it? What had his manner been like, had he had this unruffled self-confidence, before he had been built up by the naïve and generous love of his Gillian? And hadn't he been markedly unwilling to put Richard in touch with any old friends of his in England?

'Do you really think she's right?' Chilmark asked.

'All in all, I suppose not,' Richard admitted reluctantly. 'But I wish there were some way you could just prove you aren't Paul Clyro. It would make everything so much easier for everyone.'

'I wish I could too.' Chilmark refilled Richard's glass. 'I'll give the matter some thought and see if I can come up with something. Are you meaning to stay long in Madeira?'

'I haven't decided,' Richard said.

'Now you're here, I shouldn't hurry away. You should see some more of the island. The mountains. The North Coast. All completely different from here. It's a fascinating place, because the mountains are so steep and at the same time so fertile that you can get the most fantastic variations in the vegetation within minutes, almost. If that sort of thing interests you.'

'Why don't we all go off for the day tomorrow?' Gillian said eagerly. 'Have you anything else on tomorrow, Richard? We might go, say, by Encumesda over to Porto Moniz and swim there and have lunch and come back along the coast road. You'd love it.'

'I'm sorry,' Chilmark said swiftly, 'but I've something else on. A hard day's work. But another day perhaps.'

'Thanks,' Richard said, 'I'd be delighted.'

It was replying to a polite non-invitation with a polite non-acceptance. He finished his wine and stood up to go.

Chilmark asked how he intended to get back to Funchal, and when Richard said by bus, Chilmark said he would be glad to drive Richard down to the bus-stop. Richard replied that he would like to walk, to stroll about the village and look at the harbour. Chilmark came to the gate to see him off, followed by Gillian, who put her arm around his waist and leant affectionately against him.

Richard found his way back to the small square above the harbour, but it was not by the same route as his taxi had taken. To reach the square itself he found himself walking along a narrow street with a low, thick wall on one side of it, below which the waves rolled in placidly on to a narrow strip of the black, pebbled beach, and on the other side a row of small, whitewashed cottages, their plaster cracked and their eaves gap-toothed where tiles had fallen. The windows were green-shuttered and had washing slung from window to window against the stained walls in a bright, ragged scalloping.

There was a stink too.

At first it made Richard think of cattle-droppings, then he realized that it was human. It came out of the open doors and hung horribly on the air around him. The feeling that this village was a place of great picturesque charm began to evaporate. He saw it as a place inhabited by poverty, dirt and probably disease, and with Anglo-Saxon squeamishness on encountering these things, he recoiled and began to walk rather faster towards the square at the end of the little winding street.

As he did so hordes of children once more erupted out of nowhere and surrounded him. Their little hands at the ends of thin little arms came writhing around him, as if he were in a pit of snakes, and their voices piped shrilly, '*Escudo! Escudo!*'

He tried to walk on. They blocked his path. Their faces were beautiful, small, dark, delicate-featured, alive and smiling.

'*Escudo!*' they cried. '*Escudo!*'

They were like insects swarming around a juicy piece of meat.

Richard put a hand into his pocket, thinking that he could buy off the nuisance with a little largesse. With a sense of shock his hand encountered a bony little hand that had got into his pocket ahead of him. He slapped the hand away. A little girl with the face of an angel shrieked what were obviously obscenities at him, and her hand made another dive for his pocket. At the same moment another even smaller child began to explore the pocket on his other hip.

A feeling of almost frightened helplessness flooded him. In God's name, what were you to do when you were attacked by little children? You didn't hit children, did you? Not according to all the rules by which Richard had been brought up. You didn't box their ears, or grab two of their heads and bang them together. Or did you? At what point did your self-control snap and your strong adult hands lash out at the squirming, shrieking mass?

'*Escudo! Escudo!*' they shouted.

Then all at once they abandoned him. He thought for a moment, as he realized that he was free of them, that, as children will, they had suddenly become tired of plaguing him. Then he saw that they had simply spotted other prey. Another man had entered the street from the direction of the square and was walking towards Richard. He was a smallish man of about fifty, dressed in brown cotton slacks and a green and white striped shirt. His head was bald, he had only the faintest of eyebrows, and his whole face had a pale, shiny, hairless look. The shouting beggar-horde of children engulfed him.

He spoke to them softly.

Richard could not hear what he said, or even in what language he spoke, but the children appeared to understand it. There was a break in their clamour and they drew a little away from him.

He spoke again.

They drew farther away. Then, without any communication between them, they seemed all to arrive simultaneously at the agreement that they had urgent business elsewhere, and went running off towards the square. The little street was silent.

The bald man smiled at Richard.

'There's a language everybody understands,' he said.

'As a matter of interest,' Richard said, 'what language was it?'

The man raised the camera that he was carrying and aimed it down the street, clicking it at the peeling walls, the green shutters, the loops of washing.

'Technically speaking, it was, I suppose, English,' he said. 'But an infant in arms would have understood it. I was simply cursing them, you see. I don't mean swearing at them. They'd be used to that. I mean I was literally calling hellfire down on their heads. And they knew it.'

'A nice trick, if you can do it,' Richard said. 'Do you have to believe in hellfire yourself to be able to do it successfully?'

'D'you know, I've never thought about that,' the man said. 'Perhaps you do. I was brought up on fire and brimstone myself, which perhaps predisposes me to believe in the power of evil. Which, in the modern world, isn't difficult.' He aimed his camera at the harbour, the jagged black rocks, the bright blue boats. 'Charming spot,' he said.

'If you can stand the smell,' Richard said.

The man sniffed thoughtfully. 'D'you know, I hadn't noticed it? But now you mention it, yes, it is pretty strong. The smell of poverty. Well, there are worse ones. Corruption, for instance.' The shutter clicked again. 'Haven't we met somewhere?' he said. 'I seem to know your face.'

'We came out on the same plane yesterday,' Richard said.

'Ah yes, and I think I noticed you at dinner in the hotel. Are you on your way back there now, by any chance? I've a car in the square. I could give you a lift back, if that would be any use to you.'

'That's very kind,' Richard said. 'Thank you.

'You'll have to face my driving, of course. Are you a brave man? I hired the car this morning and I'm only just beginning to get accustomed to driving on the wrong side of the road. However, I can promise, I'm not reckless, I go at a snail's pace.'

He had turned and they were walking towards the square. 'Of course, some people's nerves won't stand that. They don't feel safe unless they're in a hurry. In flight, you might say.'

'I never hurry unless I've got to,' Richard answered.

'That's what I thought, somehow,' the man said, and it sounded almost as if, improbably, this were a subject to which he had devoted some consideration. 'A step at a time. Look before you leap. Very wise, on the whole. There's a disadvantage to it, however. Just occasionally you find yourself subject to ungovernable impulses – who doesn't? – and you discover then that you've had no practice in dealing with them. So you do astonishing things that are really quite out of character. Like, for instance, dashing out suddenly to Madeira. By the way, my name's Codsall. Arthur Codsall.'

'Mine's Richard Hedon.'

'Not connected with the Hedons in Farcet Street?'

'Yes, I'm one of them.'

'Well, well,' Arthur Codsall said. 'What a coincidence. That's why I felt I'd seen you before, I expect. I often drop in there to browse around.'

They had reached the square and Codsall had unlocked the door of a pale green Fiat that was parked in the shade of the acacias, where the same group of men who had been there when Richard arrived in his taxi were still lounging and chatting.

Richard never quite knew what made him say what he did as he got into the car beside Codsall. But a sharp, startled sense of recognition had come to him, as positive as what an animal must feel when it picks up a remembered trail.

'Shall we drop the nonsense?' he said. 'You feel you've seen me before because you've been following me. As you've been following Mrs Clyro. Now suppose you tell me what it's all about.'

Chapter Seven

There was a pause. Then Codsall said thoughtfully, 'Oh.'

He looked straight ahead. He started the car. It moved out of the square and on to the main road back to Funchal.

'Well,' he said after a little while, and then fell silent, as if all had been said that it was necessary to say.

The silence defeated Richard. He had meant to say no more himself. He had meant to let silence work for him. But the other man had employed its services first. When they had driven on for some distance, with Codsall's profile motionless beside him, Richard could not control himself.

'What *is* it all about?' he demanded. 'I assume your interest in me is purely because of my connection with Mrs Clyro, but why have you been following her?'

'Now you can't seriously expect me to explain that, if you don't already know,' Codsall answered in a very reasonable tone of voice.

'I don't know, and nor does she,' Richard said.

'I wouldn't be too sure of that,' Codsall replied.

'I *am* sure.'

'Why?'

'Because of what I know of her.'

'You never knew her husband, did you?'

'No.'

'No,' the other man echoed and nodded, as if he were checking some item on a list, putting a tick against it. Then he again fell silent.

Beginning to get angrier, aware that it was unwise to let this happen, that if he did he might suddenly find himself in deeper water than he was prepared for, Richard again could not make himself let the silence last. 'You know you've been frightening her atrociously.'

'I'm sorry,' Codsall said.

'Far from being sorry, it's what you intended.'

'What makes you think that?'

'Simply that you've wanted her to know she was being

followed. If you hadn't wanted that, you'd have seen to it that she didn't know.'

'Oh dear, you seem to take me for a superman,' Codsall said with a rueful smile. 'I'm not as clever as all that, unfortunately. I'd like to be, but really I was just unlucky. I was spotted quite early on. Of course someone else ought to have been put on to the job, but we're shockingly understaffed, you know. Odd, really, when you think of all the bright young people there are around who are simply longing for a chance to do some cloak-and-dagger stuff. But so few applicants are really suitable.'

'All right, laugh at me,' Richard said, 'but I still believe you've been deliberately intimidating Mrs Clyro, and she's not in a state to stand it. It's an abominable thing to do. I feel like writing to my member of parliament about the invasion of privacy by you people. Anyway, what do you want with her? Do you think she can lead you to her husband? You couldn't be more wrong. She's hunting for him desperately herself. And why do you want him? As I've understood it, there was never a breath of suspicion against him.'

'Never a breath?' Codsall said. 'Is that what you believe, Mr Hedon? Never a *breath* . . . ? Wasn't it because of that cold breath down his neck that he vanished?'

'Perhaps, but that was mainly because he'd got neurotic about it.'

'You think you saw him this morning, don't you?'

'I'm not at all sure that I did.'

'Is that the truth?'

'Yes, it's the truth. I have my doubts. I think the man I saw may simply be Gavin Chilmark.'

'Well, that's interesting. Because you came here expecting him to be Clyro, didn't you?'

'Look – !' Richard suddenly became explosive. 'What right have you to question me like this? Who do you think you are?'

'Officially I've no right to ask you anything at all,' Codsall said. 'Not at the present time. But it could save both of us a lot of bother with red tape if you'd just tell me what I want to know.'

'Mr Codsall, so far as I'm concerned, I'll be happy if you strangle in your red tape.'

'But you're looking for Clyro, aren't you? His wife sent you. Oh, the patience of these women. Do you remember the Mac-Lean story, how long and quietly she waited? Hazel Clyro's just the type that knows how to wait. Tell me, don't you think she's simply using you at the moment to communicate with her husband somehow? Perhaps you yourself don't even understand how. Perhaps you haven't even been given the message yet. Something from him to her. Something for you to take back with you. That's the only sense I can make of what's happened.'

Richard became aware of a sudden chill along his nerves. For an instant the bright blue of the sky became filmed with shadows. Suppose there were truth, even the smallest grain of it, in what the man said . . .

Codsall went on, 'I don't think I suspect you of anything intentionally traitorious. But you must admit you've done some very odd things lately, such as rushing off all of a sudden to Madeira, when your normal habit is to plan your holiday carefully some time ahead, you favour the West of Scotland, and you're generally fairly economical about it. Yet a few days ago you seem to have had one of those ungovernable impulses we were talking about, which makes people act quite out of character. Or it seems out of character if one doesn't understand all the circumstances. As I don't. But I'd like to. Tell me, what makes you doubt that Chilmark is Clyro, when you were expecting him to be?'

Richard had an intense dislike of losing his temper. At the time, of course, there was often pleasure in it, it could give you a sense of abounding certitude, of irresistible power. But the reaction that came later was generally horrible. He turned his head away, looking out at the sea and the long slope down to it, covered with the glossy, fringed foliage of bananas.

Codsall gave a sigh and said, 'I'm sorry. I was going too fast. Perhaps another time . . . How about a drink when we get back to the hotel? I won't talk about Clyro or his wife. That's a promise.'

But he would work at worming his way farther into Richard's confidence, Richard thought. Everything that this man said or did would be calculated.

However, a certain curiosity about him made Richard agree to meet him presently in the bar, and what they talked about was Madeira itself, and foreign travel generally, just as if they were two tourists who had happened to get talking over their drinks, or else two of the scientists or civil servants whom Richard had met at the Ottershaws' party, which had been the beginning of all this.

It made him reflect that the expenses of Codsall's journey were almost certainly being paid by the state, whereas Richard himself was having to pay his own, and the few days that he was intending to spend here would make a bigger hole in his bank balance than the two or three weeks that he had intended to spend in Scotland. And that brought him to the question of how Codsall had known of his habit of going to Scotland, as well as so much about Richard's temperament.

It made him feel again like bursting out with some acrimonious remarks about the freedom of the individual, the right to privacy, the degradation of being followed about, investigated, spied on. Instead, he bought Codsall another drink. Presently, very amicably, they parted, each going to his separate table in the dining-room for lunch.

Afterwards Richard stretched out on his bed and thought about Gavin Chilmark.

Was he or was he not Clyro?

The evidence of the photograph was inconclusive. If it had been taken of the man now called Chilmark, then he had altered a great deal since it had been done. But some people do alter a great deal between youth and early middle age. Witness, Jerome Ottershaw. And some personalities change a great deal if circumstances change. Gavin Chilmark could not be described as what Jeannie Ottershaw had called an AEIOU, but he might have been helped to grow out of it by discovering that instead of having to live his life as a second-rate scientist, always in the shadow of others, he was capable of living it as a successful thriller writer.

But it was certain that he did not intend to admit that he was Paul Clyro, even if he was. So what was Richard to do about it?

In the heat of the afternoon he drifted off to sleep with the question unanswered.

When he woke presently he had another swim, then later ordered a large gin and dry martini to be sent to his room and drank it on his balcony, mainly because he did not want to be trapped in the bar into another chat with Arthur Codsall. The balcony was in shade now and the air felt fresh and cool, with the first veil of the early twilight forming over its brightness.

The telephone rang.

He went into his bedroom and picked it up.

'Gavin Chilmark speaking,' a voice said. 'Just an idea. Would you like it if Gillian took you a drive across the island over to Porto Moniz and so on tomorrow? I'd like to go myself, but as I told you, I'll be working. But if you'd like her to collect you in the morning, she'd be delighted.'

'That's extraordinarily good of her,' Richard said.

'Sure? No need to go if you aren't really enthusiastic. But she always loves having something to do when I start pounding my typewriter.'

'I'd love to go.'

'Good. Then suppose she picks you up about nine-thirty? You'll need most of the day. There's a nice little hotel over there on the North Coast where you can have lunch. And when you get back, perhaps you'd come in for a drink and a meal here.'

'Thank you, that's very kind.'

'Oh, we'll both look forward to it. You made such a nice change in our day. Perhaps you can think up some more nice surprises for us tomorrow.' A slight chuckle came to Richard over the line. 'We'll see you tomorrow then.'

Chilmark rang off, leaving Richard to wonder if the invitation had been simple hospitality and as kind as it sounded, or if there had been something else behind it.

Returning to the balcony, he sat watching some fishing boats move slowly out to sea, their lights shining like dim stars scattered on the quiet surface of the ocean.

What possible dubious motive could Chilmark have had in suggesting the drive? Gillian was not the most discreet person in the world, and Chilmark must have known that Richard would be certain to see what he could get out of her. So did that mean that she knew nothing that could be useful to Richard, or else, quite simply, that there was nothing to know.

Richard finished his drink and went to the dining-room.

He did not see Codsall at dinner, yet Richard knew when he came in, for although he was sitting at a window table with his back to the room, the English couple at the table next to his kept up a running commentary on everything that went on within their range of vision. They spoke so clearly, both in flat, carrying voices, that it sounded as if they must believe that no one there, instead of at least ninety-nine per cent of the diners, spoke English. They both looked about seventy and were small and bony, and had curiously similar, bitter little faces.

'I had that yesterday,' the man said, reading from the menu. He sounded bored and discouraged at the thought.

'Yes,' his wife agreed, 'you had that yesterday.'

'I liked it, didn't I?' he asked dubiously.

'Yes, you said you liked it.'

'I'll have it now, I think.' Better the dangers of foreign cooking that you had once survived than new and perhaps more deadly ones.

'Then I'll have it too . . . Oh look, there's that honeymoon couple. She's got still another dress on this evening. What show-offs they both are, acting as if no one else had ever had a love affair before them. Look, they're practically rubbing noses over their wine-glasses. I call it disgusting. I give that marriage two years at the outside. And there's that young man with the long hair, the one all by himself with the little boy. He looks the kind who'd beat you up as soon as look at you. And the boy's defective, anyone can see that. The father does try to look after him though, I'll say that for him. A sad story behind that, I shouldn't wonder. Wife probably wouldn't face her responsibilities and went off and left him. That's what they're like nowadays. And there's that man who likes his wine. Another bottle – did you see that, he's just ordered *another* bottle?'

'And there's that man with the queer eyes,' her husband said, 'the one without eyelashes.'

'Yes, they make you think of a lizard's, don't they? I don't like the look of him.'

'He always seems to be watching us, for some reason. What is there peculiar about us?'

'I don't think it's us he's watching. I think it's the young man at the next table. What d'you suppose a young man like that is doing all by himself in a place like this? There are plenty of pretty girls around. I don't think it's healthy.'

The stream of venom spurted inconsequently on throughout the meal. After it, the soft murmur of surf on rocks that Richard could hear faintly from his balcony seemed gentleness itself. Again, sated with the day's sunshine, he went to bed early.

In the morning Gillian arrived punctually at half past nine. Codsall was in the lobby when Richard went out to meet her, and said a cheerful good-morning.

Gillian was driving a new Rover 3500 and was wearing a dress of turquoise linen with a bold dash of the island embroidery down the front of it. Her fair hair was held smoothly back from her forehead by a narrow gold band and she had on big, dark glasses. Instead of looking seventeen, as she had yesterday, she looked twenty-seven and serenely accustomed to opulence.

That, at least, was Richard's impression until she began to talk. Then he sensed a tension in her that had not been there the day before. The words came too fast, too eagerly to sound natural.

'You've got your swimming things, haven't you?' she said. 'We're going up into the mountains, then down to the coast and we'll have a swim there. Gavin says I'm to tell you he really wishes he could come, he did so enjoy meeting you yesterday, but he's behind on the weekly schedule he's set himself because he went out on one of the fishing boats the other night – he loves doing that – so he'll be writing all day. D'you like our car? It's the first new car I've ever possessed and it was the first thing Gavin gave me when he began to get rich. And it's all mine, he says. He goes on driving the old Austin. That's partly because he doesn't like change, and he's not at all mechanically minded, so having got accustomed to the old car, he sticks to it.'

'What did he do before he decided to be a drop-out in Madeira?' Richard asked.

The car had glided out of the hotel drive and taken the same direction as the taxi had taken the day before.

'He was a journalist,' Gillian answered.

'On what paper?'

'Oh, he was a freelance. He wrote about anything and every-thing, gardening, cookery, environmental pollution, travel, poli-tics, short stories sometimes – just about anything that he could read up on and sell.'

'Science?' Richard asked.

'Of course, who doesn't? He's one of those people with almost – what do you call it? – total recall. He can read a thing about something he knows hardly anything about, and remember it and dish it up in different words with a different sort of approach, and sell it, and gradually start to be quoted as an authority. I think he'd have been wonderful on television, if he hadn't got his funny wink. So authoritative, you know, and sure of himself, when really he doesn't know the first thing about what he's talking about.'

'The wink's Bell's palsy, isn't it?' Richard said. 'How long ago did he get it?'

'Oh, a couple of years, I think. He'd had it quite recently when I first met him. It was much worse then than it is now. His face was completely lop-sided and his one eyelid hardly moved at all. So when I saw him first across a café in Funchal, I thought he was winking at me and I winked back. And ie looked so hurt and upset, I realized I'd done something awful and he couldn't help winking. So I went up to him and apolo-gized. And so here we are.'

Richard wondered how many other people would have had the courage to apologize to a perfect stranger who hadn't been able to help winking at them.

'He was living on his freelancing then, was he?' he asked.

'Well, just. He was just getting by. Of course, he could do his writing anywhere, but he'd come abroad to get away from that awful wife of his. He hadn't decided to make his home here. I think if we hadn't met he'd soon have moved on some-where else. But we did meet, and we fell in love, and I had a little money of my own, so we didn't have to worry about whether or not he could keep me, and now I expect we'll stay here for ever. We've been so happy . . . '

But the tension was still in her voice and in the small, strong hands on the wheel.

'Today you aren't happy,' Richard said. 'Yesterday you really were, but today you aren't. What's the matter, Gillian?'

'Nothing's the matter.'

'Something is.'

'Well, everyone has their ups and downs, don't they? I didn't sleep very well.'

'Is that really all?'

'Of course it is.'

'If this drive is a bore for you, we don't really have to go, you know. If you'd just drop me back at the hotel . . .'

'It isn't a bore. I'm looking forward to it. But if you want me to take you back, of course I will.'

'I don't.'

'Then what are we arguing about?'

'That thing called happiness.'

'Oh yes. Well, of course, my poor aunts were fit to be tied when I told them I was staying here, but I was happy for the first time in my life . . . Oh, look, did you see that?'

She had waved a hand as they passed at a short, steep incline, a narrow roughly cobbled road, that went up a hillside, apparently to nowhere.

'Well,' she went on, 'there's a little church at the top. You can't see it from down here. And the women hereabouts go up there to pray for their husbands' safe return when they go abroad to try to make money. A lot of them go away to Venezuela or Brazil, and sometimes, of course, they never come back. But if they do, and particularly if they come back rich, and can afford to build a fine new house for themselves, with a garage and everything, then the women go back to that church to offer up thanks, and they climb up there, all the way up over those awful cobbles, *on their knees*. Think of that!'

'I see,' Richard said.

'Do you?'

'Yes, and what's more, I can see you doing it.'

At the same moment he had a sudden vision of Anne Damerel doing it. She would have done that and how much more if they had ever sent Peter safely back to her out of the hospital.

But Richard was not sure if he could see Hazel doing it for Paul Clyro, if he ever returned to her, rich or poor, out of his ambiguous non-existence. And why should she? There were times when pride should stop you dropping to your knees, whatever there might be in the way of thankfulness in your heart.

'Do a lot of the men go abroad?' he asked.

'Oh yes, and some of them, the illiterate ones, which generally means the older ones, of course, who can't get permits to work abroad – they go off to Spain and then jump ship and make their way across the border into France, and generally aren't heard of again.'

'So this isn't a paradise for everyone.'

'Is there anywhere on earth that is? Look up there.'

She pointed at a cliff rising steeply up from the side of the road. Along a ledge near the top of the cliff there was what looked like a dump of corrugated iron, wooden planking and tar-paper.

'There are caves up there,' she said, 'and people live in them. People have always lived in them, I suppose ever since the island was discovered. And one day the Government came along and thought this wasn't a very good thing and they built a lot of new houses, just like the council houses at home. They're small and neat and comfortable and cheap. And the cave-dwellers moved into them out of the caves. And what d'you think happened? Immediately a lot of other people moved into the caves. I don't know where they'd been living before. But if they were moved out, I'm sure there'd be more people who'd move in. And some of them, at least for a time, would think the caves were paradise. As 7 Rua Ponte Nova has been for me. Gavin's a wonderful, wonderful man. Of course it's lovely having money too all of a sudden, but it isn't what counts. Gavin's absolutely all on earth I want.'

'Tell me some more about your aunts,' Richard said. 'Were you very unhappy with them?'

'Oh, not *unhappy*.' She swung the car to the right, away from the sea, along a road that ran parallel to the stony bed of a dried up river into a rocky opening into the mountains, which loomed up ahead, one behind another, higher and higher. 'They were terribly good to me, and I think they were really very fond of me. You see, my mother committed suicide soon after I was born, I think just because she simply couldn't cope, and I hadn't any official father – I was illegitimate, in other words – and my mother's sisters took me on. They were wonderful, really, because, for one thing, they weren't rich, but they'd never use any of my mother's money for me. They said that was for me when I grew up. So I owe them a terrible lot. But honestly, they were so *odd*. I always felt different from all the other children I met, and I never understood why. I thought my life was normal, but really . . . ! '

Her laugh rang out. It sounded as if her tension were beginning to be dispelled by her own chatter.

'I'll tell you the story of the trifles, and you'll see what I mean. You see, they were much older than my mother, so they always seemed ancient to me, and they used to stay in bed till midday, then not go to bed till three in the morning. And drink! It was ages, of course, before I understood about that, I thought it was what everybody's aunts were like and that everything would be different if I had a mother. And they used to make me do the oddest things. Once, this time I'm telling you about, they made me get up at one a.m. on a winter's night and go over to a neighbour to ask her if she'd any milk to spare because they'd just started making trifles for the church bazaar next day, and they'd forgotten to order any extra milk for them. The neighbour wasn't at all pleased, and she said she hadn't any milk anyway, so the three of us, my aunts and I, got three taxis, and we spent the night going to all the all-night dairies and the milk machines in the neighbourhood, buying up all the milk we could get. Then they made two enormous trifles. And next day at the bazaar they asked the vicar if they could buy their own trifles back, because they'd put a bottle of Bristol Cream in them.'

Her laughter again bubbled out spontaneously.

Then abruptly the amusement went out of her voice.

'Actually, I've never forgotten the expression I saw on that neighbour's face while I was talking to her,' she said. 'She was exasperated and she was sorry for me, and she was trying not to laugh outright. I think it was then it dawned on me I'd have to escape. And then we came abroad for the sake of my education, which cost those two poor old darlings the earth, and I met Gavin and walked out on them. Of course they said, "like mother, like daughter," which is probably true, because human patterns do repeat themselves endlessly, don't they? But for the first time in my life I began to feel normal. Just ordinary. An ordinary sort of girl with a home of her own and a man to love. It was such a wonderful feeling . . . ' She shot a sidelong glance at Richard, then swung the car round a bend and up on to a dizzily steep zigzag of a hill, with a ravine of tumbled rock beneath it. 'Your Margaret isn't going to take all that away from me. And you don't want her to, do you? So perhaps we should get together on it.'

'I don't know anyone called Margaret,' he answered.

As he said it, he glanced back at the earth that tilted away behind them, and saw, just starting up the zigzag, a hundred yards behind them, a pale green Fiat.

Richard said nothing about it to Gillian, but all the way across the island, he saw that the green car stayed about the same distance behind them. If Gillian noticed it, she appeared to find nothing remarkable about it. There were not many places where the other car could have passed them. The road was so steep, so narrow, and with so many sharp bends, that for cars to proceed in a patient, slow-moving procession, making no attempt at passing, was normal.

The road wound upwards into a region of pines and eucalyptus, where the air was richly aromatic and there were huge clumps of blue hydrangeas at the roadside. Then, for a time, there was cloud, damp and chilly, all around them. Gillian told Richard that they would soon be above it and soon they were, in sunshine of aching brilliance. The vegetation was much sparser here, bare grass with trees which she said were actually giant heathers, dotted over the mountainside. In the distance, dark, jagged mountain peaks swam above the steaming cauldron of fog, looking theatrical and insubstantial, as if they had only been painted there on the backdrop of the sky.

'They had to chop down a lot of the original pine forests during the war,' Gillian said, 'because they hadn't any other fuel, so then they planted faster growing things, like these heathers and sweet chestnuts. Of course, you know Madeira means the wooded isle, don't you? When Zarco found it, it was entirely covered in forest.'

'You seem to know a lot about the island,' Richard said.

'I read it up for Gavin when he was doing some travel articles,' she replied. 'In fact, I used to write some of them for him when he was too busy fishing.' She gave a little giggle. 'You know how you said your friend Mrs Clyro told you some of the scenes in *Taken As Red* had happened between her and her husband? Well, if she meant the love scenes, which was how I took it, it would be really very funny, because I wrote most of them. Gavin simply can't do the sex stuff at all. It comes out as wooden as if he'd never made love to a woman in his life. So when he thinks it's time for a bit of romance, he hands it over to me, and I dream away on to the paper for a couple of thousand words, and it works beautifully.'

The road had begun to descend. But this side of the island was clear of fog. The road wound down through pines to slopes where every inch where a human foot could find a toe-hold was terraced and covered in vines. At the foot of the slope the great rollers of the Atlantic came smoothly in, breaking with a roar and a fountain of spray along the rocky shore.

A level road ran parallel to the shore. The hillside on the left of the road was laced with the glittering threads of waterfalls that came weaving down, some over the road itself. Gillian stopped the car under one of them, saying she might as well give the car a free wash while she could. The water pattered on the roof like rain. A moment later she was driving into a dark stone tunnel that appeared to plunge straight into the hillside.

But almost at once they saw brightness ahead, a square of it, growing larger, and soon they emerged into sunshine once more. As they did so, Richard looked back. The lights of the Fiat were shining in the tunnel behind them.

Porto Moniz was a fishing village with a small quay, a cluster of cottages, a small hotel and two swimming pools. The pools had been formed by filling in gaps between teeth of black volcanic rock with concrete. They were eerie places. The breakers, crashing against the outer barriers, made a steady thunder and sent up jets of foam, but within the sheltering jaws of the dark reefs the water was motionless and clear.

There were cabins above the pools, where Gillian and Richard changed into their swimming things. No one else was swimming there and there was no one about but a small boy, who had given them the keys to their cabins, and who sat and watched them in the water. It was far colder here than in Funchal. The boy tossed a pebble from hand to hand and whistled a soft, monotonous tune. The Fiat, to Richard's surprise, had vanished. Arthur Codsall was not to be seen.

But he was in the dining-room in the hotel, sitting by himself, eating fried fish, when Gillian and Richard went into it for lunch after their swim.

He smiled at Richard and said, 'Ah, I thought that looked like you ahead of me. Fascinating road, wasn't it? And all these rocks here – so formidable, one can't make up one's mind if they're beautiful or rather dreadful. I own they frighten me a little. But probably I'm too easily scared. Would you and your friend care to join me?'

He had stood up and was already pulling out a chair for Gillian, who was so delighted at having found someone new to talk to, and was so quick to tell him that her name was Gillian Chilmark and that he ought to have had a swim too, because it made one feel so wonderful and hungry, and that she would have the fish and the steak, please, and, yes, some wine too, of course, that there was nothing for Richard to do but to sit down facing Codsall and endure it.

Neither of the two men talked very much during the meal, but Gillian made up for it. Soon she had told Codsall almost everything about herself that she had told Richard yesterday, that her husband was the writer of a book that had been made into a marvellous film, from which they had made lots and lots of money, only, of course, he wasn't really her husband, everybody knew that, so why pretend, and it was lovely being rich, only not as important as you might think, if you happened to be wonderfully happy anyhow.

'Happy?' Codsall said, and sounded all at once bewildered, as if it were a word he had not heard before. 'Just – happy?'

Richard grinned and said, 'I know – formidable, isn't it, rather like those rocks? It's difficult to make up one's mind if it's beautiful or rather dreadful. And it's certainly frightening.'

'I don't know what you're talking about,' Gillian said.

'Just so long as you go on not knowing,' Richard answered.

She looked with a puzzled frown from one to the other. Codsall looked down at the checked tablecloth, his lashless eyelids drooping. After a moment he gave a sigh and drank a little wine and seemed to withdraw into himself, becoming rather sadly silent.

When they emerged presently on to the terrace outside the hotel, there was a kitten playing in the sunshine. It was a very young kitten, of a smoky grey, and it had found a butterfly to stalk. The butterfly had settled, wings a-quiver, on the concrete of the terrace. The kitten did not approach it directly. First it became utterly still. Then it crept soundlessly to one side, taking cover behind one of the poles that supported the porch. There the kitten remained, its eyes never leaving the butterfly, for a full minute, no part of it moving except for the very tip of its tail. The butterfly also was still, delicate and lovely. Even the quivering of its wings had stopped. Then the kitten crept a few inches forward and waited again. The butterfly appeared unaware of it. Then all of a sudden the kitten streaked forward, the born hunter, brought into the world only a few weeks before, but with all its predatory instincts there, ready to be used. But the butterfly sailed away serenely, its escape from extinction timed to the instant. The kitten tried not to look foolish.

Gillian laughed with pleasure.

'You poor little kitten,' she said, stooping to pet the disappointed creature, which had stopped looking like a miniature tiger and seemed glad of the sympathy. 'Things aren't as easy as all that. You've such a lot to learn still, haven't you?'

Arthur Codsall began to laugh too. He laughed and laughed. It was as if, once he started, he could not stop. He was still chuckling helplessly, in little explosions like hiccups, as he said good-bye to Gillian and Richard and went off to his car.

It was early evening when they reached Vila do Bonfim again. They had not returned across the mountains, but had taken the road round the west of the island, reaching the little house in the Rua Ponte Nova as the sun was beginning to sink. The Fiat was behind them for most of the way, but in one of the villages it went past them and disappeared ahead. Arthur Codsall raised a hand in greeting as he went by.

'Oh dear, I meant to ask him in for a drink,' Gillian said, 'but now I suppose I've missed him. You're coming in for one, aren't you? And staying for a meal, Gavin said.'

'Thank you, I'm looking forward to it,' Richard answered.

'I think it's going to be stuffed aubergines. That is, if . . . ' She stopped with odd abruptness.

'Yes?' Richard said. He noticed that her hands on the wheel were tense again, as they had been at the beginning of the drive.

'I was going to say, if he hasn't simply gone on working and forgotten to cook anything.'

For some reason Richard felt sure that that was not what she had been going to say.

She added, 'In that case it'll be omelets, but I hope it's aubergines. He does them marvellously.'

They stopped at the gate. The old Austin which Gillian had said Chilmark drove was in the road outside it. The door of the house was ajar, as it had been when Richard had visited it yesterday. A bird whose unfamiliar call Richard had noticed in the hotel garden the evening before sang out suddenly, as if in warning, as they went up the path. The scent of the datura in the garden had a heavy, sickly sweetness.

Afterwards Richard was always to associate that overpowering perfume with what happened that evening.

Gillian went into the house ahead of him. She screamed. It was the most eldritch sound that Richard had ever heard. He came in rapidly behind her. The room was buzzing with flies. They circled blackly in the air, slowly and drowsily, as if satiated, and they crawled obscenely over the dead face and around the great blood-rimmed hole that had once been the winking eye of Gavin Chilmark, who sprawled stiffly in a basket chair, facing the door.

Chapter Eight

Gillian fell on her knees beside him. She clutched him round the waist, and burrowed her face into his side. Her wordless wailing went on. Her eyes were shut. Richard thought that she was not even aware of the sounds that she was making.

He took a step towards her, instinctively wanting to draw her out of her dreadful embrace. But he stopped before he touched her. He thought that a girl like Gillian, to save her sanity, probably needed to scream out her agony. Looking round the room, he saw that the sewing-machine was still on the table under the window, the ironing-board still stood in the middle of the room and a half-made dress was draped over the board, ready for the seams to be pressed. The disorder was all of the same kind as yesterday's. There were no signs of a struggle having happened in the room. Nor was there any sign of a weapon. It looked almost as if someone had walked in at the door and even before Chilmark had had time to get out of his chair, had shot him and walked out again.

Richard's thoughts went straight to Arthur Codsall.

That ambiguous man. That man, Richard felt, who could easily be capable of murder.

The light green Fiat had stayed behind Gillian's car all the way to Porto Moniz and most of the way back, but at last had passed it in one of the villages and must have driven into Vila do Bonfim ten minutes or so ahead of Gillian and Richard. That would have given Codsall time to walk quickly into the house, shoot Chilmark and leave.

Only Chilmark had the look of having been dead far longer than ten minutes. Richard reached out and touched the hand that hung over the arm of the chair. The flesh was cold and the fingers were stiff. So Codsall could not possibly have done the shooting. He had been in the hotel when Richard left it with Gillian and had been in clear view of them all day. His alibi was perfect.

Gillian's wailing changed to a noisy sobbing. Richard wondered if she would be capable of speaking if he asked her a question. He wanted to know where there was a telephone. There was none in this room. But was there one in some other room in the house or had Chilmark had to go out to telephone when he had spoken to Richard in the hotel the evening before?

He glanced again at Gillian, then thought that he might as well leave her for a little longer in the stupor of her grief while he did a little quiet exploring. Crossing the room to a door that was not the one that led into the kitchen, he went through it and found himself in a small, dark passage, at the end of which steep, narrow, cottage stairs ascended to the floor above and out of which another door opened into a little room which was obviously Chilmark's study.

There was a telephone there on a neat desk, on which there were a typewriter, a lamp, a pile of typing paper, a pile of typescript, a collection of ball-point pens and a pile of letters, under a paperweight. This was simply one of the big black pebbles from the shore. Everything was tidily arranged, as different from the living-room, dominated by Gillian and her sewing, as it could be.

The only things in the room besides the desk were one chair, a bookcase full of reference books, mostly about the police, poisons and guns as well as an encyclopedia and the *Oxford Dictionary of Quotations*, and on the wall a coloured photograph of Gillian. She was in a bright red bikini, standing, one hand on a dimpled hip, on the formidable black beach of Vila do Bonfim, and looking as if no shadow could ever darken her life. With the harsh sound of her sobbing still in his ears, Richard found it extraordinarily painful to look at the picture. He turned away from it, and looked for the telephone directory.

It was lying on top of the bookcase. But as he reached out for it, he realized that of course he would not be able to make the call to the police. It would have to be done in Portuguese. He would have to leave it to Gillian.

Returning to the living-room, he found that she had let go of the dead man and was sitting back on her heels beside the chair in which he was sprawled. Her eyes were open now and she was gazing into his shattered face with a mixture of deep tenderness and horror. Tears trickled down her cheeks and her body still shuddered with her sobbing, but the worst of the paroxysm had passed. When Richard took her gently by both hands, she passively allowed herself to be drawn to her feet. But when he tried to lead her to the study, she hung back, as if she felt that if she let her lover out of her sight, he might get up and walk away.

'But we've got to call the police, Gillian,' Richard said. 'I'm sorry, I'd do it if I could, but I can't talk the language. So you'll have to try. Do you think you can manage?'

She still resisted him.

'She did it, you know,' she said.

'She?'

'Margaret.'

'But she isn't here.'

'She is.'

He looked at her doubtfully. 'You don't mean that, do you?'

'Of course I do. She came this morning. I suppose she just came to kill him.'

'You saw her?'

She hesitated, then shook her head. 'He wouldn't let me stay. He said he had to tackle her by himself.'

'Then you knew she was coming?'

'Oh yes, she telephoned last night.'

'So that's why he got you to take me out for the day.'

She tossed her hair back from her face and began to mop at it with a screwed-up handkerchief. Her voice sounded a little steadier. 'Yes, of course. It got both of us out of the way while he saw her.'

'When did she arrive in Madeira?'

'On the late plane yesterday evening.'

'And you're sure she was Margaret?' A different nightmare fear had sprung into his mind.

'Well, she said so.' Gillian was allowing herself to be led to the study. Reaching it, she sat down at the desk and looked at the telephone with a curious air of wonderment, as if she were puzzling over how such an innocent-looking thing could have brought such devastation into her life. 'I answered the phone. I generally do, in case it's someone talking Portuguese. Gavin knew enough to get around the shops and so on, but the phone was beyond him. So I answered it, and she said, of course in English, "Can I speak to Mr Chilmark?" So I said, "Just a minute, I'll go and fetch him." And then, for some reason, I said, "Who is it speaking?" There was something about her voice that made me ask, I don't know what exactly. Ordinarily I'd just have called out, "Gavin, it's for you," and left it there for him, off the hook. But I asked who she was, and she gave a little laugh and said, "Tell him it's Margaret." So I got into an awful state and started to say, "Go away, go away, you aren't wanted here, please go away!" And then I thought after all I'd no right to do that and I'd better get Gavin . . . ' She paused. 'I'm sorry, you wanted me to call the police, didn't you? I don't know who to call. I've never had anything to do with the police here, except about our visas and so on. But I suppose I call our local *agente*, though I can't see him dealing with a murder.'

Richard just then would have preferred her to go on talking. But the police had to be informed. He waited while she fumbled through the pages of the directory, then made a call. There seemed to be a good deal of excitable talk from the other end of the line, at which Gillian became first incoherent, then almost dumb. At any moment, he thought, her self-control would snap again.

When she put the telephone down again, she turned to look at him vacantly, as if she had difficulty in remembering what they had been talking about.

He prompted her, 'You were saying you started to tell this Margaret to go away.'

Gillian looked as if she could not remember ever having said such a thing. Her thoughts had gone far away.

He tried again, 'Well, you went and fetched Gavin.'

The name brought her to herself. 'Yes, he was gardening. It wasn't quite dark yet and it was nice and cool. He liked to garden in the evenings . . . ' Her eyes filled with tears. 'We loved our bit of garden. Things grow so wonderfully here, you see such wonderful results so quickly. I'll have to leave it now, shan't I? I couldn't stay on here alone. But it's the first real home I've had, and I've a feeling I'll never have another. I mean, there are some things you can only have once in your life.'

100

Richard thought of policemen arriving at any moment, policemen who could talk to her only in Portuguese, so that he would not be able to understand what they were asking and she was answering, and he felt an intense need to find out certain things from her before they arrived. But he tried not to show impatience.

'You went and fetched Gavin,' he repeated quietly, 'and you told him that it was Margaret on the telephone. What happened then?'

She nodded. 'Yes, I told him that, and I said, "Please don't talk to her, please don't see her, please don't have anything to do with her!" I had a feeling, a sort of awful feeling, that something terrible was going to happen. I suppose I was just terribly afraid that she'd somehow get him away from me. Because, in spite of all the things he used to say about her, I never felt absolutely sure there wasn't a bit of him that went on loving her. And when I told him she was there, wanting to talk to him, he swore and said he didn't want to talk to her, but then he said, "Oh, I suppose I'd better, but don't worry, I won't have her coming here." So he came inside to the telephone and I stayed out in the garden, in case he should think I was eavesdropping and didn't trust him. And after a few minutes he came out and said, "She's coming here tomorrow morning. There are some things she seems to think we ought to talk over. Divorce, money and so on. But there's no need for you to see her. You'd sooner not, wouldn't you?" So I said of course I'd sooner not, though the truth was, you know, I'd sooner have been there, to see what she was like and to – well, to make sure she didn't get at him. But I knew he wanted me out of the way, so I said I didn't want to meet her and Gavin said, "Suppose you take that man Hedon off to Porto Moniz for the day," and I agreed. So Gavin telephoned you and suggested the trip.'

An adequate explanation, Richard thought, of the state of tension that Gillian had been in when she had picked him up at his hotel in the morning, and of the return of the mood on their way back to Vila do Bonfim.

'And she was to arrive here soon after you left?' he asked.

Gillian nodded.

'Did he tell you where she's staying?'

'No, just that she'd rung up from Funchal.'

'These things that he used to say about her – what were they?'

'Oh, that she was cold and selfish and never loved him, but only pretended she did, and how she'd never taken any interest in his work and so on, and that it had taken him years to understand what a sham his marriage was, and – and that he'd never known what honest love was till he met me. And of course I believed it – I mean, I do believe it – except that sometimes I used to get the feeling that the way he talked about her was just a sort of revenge for some awful hurt she'd given him. Been unfaithful, perhaps, when it mattered to him terribly that he should be the only person she ever thought about. Oh, I don't know what it was. But somehow I used to have awful feelings that if she ever tried to get him back, after he'd had all this time to get over whatever she'd done to him, she might – well, he might find I wasn't what he really wanted.'

'Did he ever tell you what she looked like?'

She thought deeply, then all at once began to cry violently again. Between he sobs she hiccuped, 'He said she was beautiful – terribly beautiful – he said – he said I could never have any idea how beautiful she was – when she was young – and how she – how she got even more beautiful as she got older.'

She began to wail again, her whole body shaking. Richard went out hurriedly in search of brandy.

He found some in the kitchen, brought it to her and almost forced some between her chattering teeth. Then he eased her gently out of the chair, moved it to a corner of the small room and sat her down in it again. She let him do it without any obvious awareness of what was happening. When he knelt down in front of the desk and began to open one drawer after another and go rapidly through them, she only watched him vaguely, as if she found nothing surprising about his behaviour.

The drawers were not very full, and, like the top of the desk, were very tidy. Chilmark must have been a very orderly man. One drawer held stationery, another letters, another contracts with all his publishers, English and foreign, another a cheque book, a bank book, and receipted bills. It was in this fourth drawer that Richard found what he was looking for, Chilmark's passport.

102

Taking it out, he laid it and Paul Clyro's passport, side by side, on the top of the desk. There was no question about it, the photographs in them were of two different men. So Gavin Chilmark was not Paul Clyro.

Not that Richard would have liked to have to swear which of the two photographs was the more like the dead man in the other room. For neither showed a bearded face, and neither showed signs of the paralysis that had affected the dead man. The two looked much of an age, and both had longish faces with high, narrow foreheads, and both were said in the passports to be six foot one, with light brown hair, grey eyes and no distinguishing marks. But there was really not the faintest resemblance between them. Apart from the fact that Clyro had worn his hair rather long, and Chilmark his cropped short, there was something far more arresting about Chilmark's face than Clyro's, something far more forceful and intense. Even in the expressionless passport photographs, Chilmark looked far the more powerful personality.

But there was a kind of bitterness, almost a sneer, in his face, which had been quite lacking in that of the easy-going man whom Richard had met in this house the day before. But that was easily explained by what Gillian had told him of Chilmark's relations with his wife. Gillian herself had erased the bitterness.

Richard returned Chilmark's passport to the drawer and Clyro's to his pocket. Hazel Clyro's idea that the two men must be the same one was a preposterous mare's nest. Richard's private nightmare died a comfortable death. For if Chilmark could not be Clyro, then the woman who had come to see him that morning could not be Hazel. Margaret Chilmark had an identity of her own.

When the police came, two men in grey cotton uniforms, with truncheons on their hips, Gillian chattered to them at length in Portuguese in a voice so shrill as to be only just short of hysteria. Richard could not guess what she was saying, but when the men had listened and asked a few questions, then gone back to the living-room obviously waiting for someone more senior to arrive, she said, 'I didn't tell them anything about that man Clyro whom you came looking for yesterday,

103

because mixing him up with Gavin was all such nonsense anyway. Gavin couldn't be anybody but Gavin. So you needn't worry.'

'How did you explain what I was doing here?' Richard asked.

'I simply said you and Gavin met in the village yesterday and he brought you home for a drink. It's the sort of thing he'd do. A fellow Englishman and all. They believe it. I told them too you'd been with me all day, so you couldn't possibly have anything to do with what happened here.'

'Only unfortunately there's someone besides you and me in Funchal who knows why I really came,' Richard said.

'Who's that?'

'The man we had lunch with at Porto Moniz. Arthur Codsall.'

'How does he know it?'

'He and I met down by the harbour yesterday and he gave me a lift back into Funchal. And he turned out to be as interested in Paul Clyro as I am. He knows I came here looking for him.'

She made a gesture of brushing away what he had said as if it were one of the black flies circling in the air.

'It doesn't matter. All they've got to do is find Margaret.'

'You're sure Margaret killed him?'

'How could it be anyone else? Wouldn't that be too strange? Margaret comes to see him and on just that day somebody else decides to shoot my poor darling Gavin – that's nonsense. Of course it was Margaret. She wanted revenge.'

'Just when he'd started to make money and there might have been some advantage to her in a simple divorce?'

'You don't think about money if it's revenge you want.'

'But if it was she who was unfaithful first, if it was really he who'd wanted revenge on her, as you said . . . ' He stopped. Gillian was not attending to him, and he knew that she was in no state to listen to a logical argument.

He left her and went out into the garden. It was dark now and the scent of the datura seemed heavier than ever. The lights of the village, densely clustered down by the harbour, more sparsely higher up the hillside, shone brightly in the clear night air. Richard wondered how safe it would be to stick to

104

the story that Gillian had told about him. Might not Arthur Codsall have his own reasons for keeping quiet? If Richard had felt that he could rely on that, he would have felt inclined to repeat what Gillian had said. But could he guess what Codsall would do? Obviously not. On the whole, Richard thought, it might be simplest in the end to tell the complicated truth. At least he would wait to make up his mind until he had seen what sort of man turned up to take charge.

The *Chefe da Policia Judiciaria*, who presently arrived from Funchal with a number of other policemen and a doctor, was a shortish, slender man with smooth dark hair, big, melancholy eyes and a thin, fine-boned face. He wore a lightweight fawn suit, a snowy shirt and shoes with thick rubber soles on which he moved about quite soundlessly. He was soft-voiced and spoke excellent English. His name was Raposo. While his men, in the living-room, took photographs, dusted the room for fingerprints and at last moved the body on to a stretcher and covered it, he had a long talk with Gillian in the little study. Richard would have remained in the garden until he was wanted if the police cars in the road had not quickly collected a crowd of neighbours, with the inescapable children among them, who came as close to the house as the police would let them, their eyes brilliant with excitement in their vivid, bandit faces. So Richard retreated to the kitchen, helped himself to some brandy, and waited to be summoned.

More than once, while he was waiting, he heard Gillian's voice raised suddenly in one of her attacks of anguished wailing, and he wondered if he ought to go to the study to make sure that she was not being bullied. But the voice that spoke to her when her own grew quiet again sounded consoling rather than threatening. At last she came out of the room and ran upstairs. Richard was invited to go into the study.

A second chair had been brought in and the *Senhor Chefe* waved Richard to it. He was asked his name, his home address, his occupation, and when he had arrived in Madeira.

'The day before yesterday,' Richard replied to the last question.

'And on your very first morning here you came to Vila do Bonfim,' Raposo said in his soft, careful English. 'May I ask what brought you? I know the village is famed for its beauty, but in your place I should probably have spent a quiet day swimming and lying in the sun, or exploring Funchal. So perhaps you had a special reason for coming.'

He looked thoughtfully at Richard, and Richard looked thoughtfully back. After only the shortest of hesitations, he made up his mind to tell the truth to the quiet little man.

'Yes, I had a reason,' he said. 'I wanted to see Gavin Chilmark.'

'Then you did not meet him just by chance.'

'No, I came to this house, looking for him. If Mrs Chilmark told you I met him in the village by chance, I think it's because she doesn't really understand my reason for coming. She doesn't believe in it.'

The dark head nodded. 'She is not, of course, Mrs Chilmark, but Miss Acheson.'

With surprise, Richard realized that this was the first time that he had heard Gillian's name.

Raposo went on, 'I am sure you knew that. She is very frank about the matter. She has told us that Mrs Margaret Chilmark came here this morning to see her husband, who deserted her some years ago. I have telephoned Funchal to see if there is any record of her coming. Also, if so, in what hotel she is staying. You have not met this Mrs Chilmark yourself?'

'No,' Richard said.

'Your reason for coming is not concerned with her?'

'No.'

'May I ask you then to explain it to me?'

'I came because I thought Gavin Chilmark might really be a man called Paul Clyro,' Richard said. 'I want to find Paul Clyro.'

'Ah. You are a detective?'

'No, I'm a friend of Clyro's wife. I'm trying to find him for her.'

'Tell me about this man.'

'I've never met him,' Richard said. 'I can't tell you anything about him at first hand. But like Chilmark, he deserted his wife two years ago – that's to say, he disappeared then. There are some curious circumstances about his disappearance. He walked out of his home one morning to go to work, taking nothing with him, no clothes, no money, no passport, and he's never been seen since. I think most people believe he's dead, killed in some accident, or even murdered and his body concealed. But his wife is sure he's alive.'

'What was it that made you think Mr Chilmark might be Mr Clyro?'

'Mrs Clyro thought so. She read Gavin Chilmark's book, *Taken As Red*, and saw the film that was made from it, and she's certain that no one but her husband could have written it.'

'I have read this book,' Raposo said. 'I was interested in the work of a resident of Madeira. It is amusing, I thought.'

'Yes, quite amusing,' Richard agreed.

'But why did Mrs Clyro think no one but her husband could have written it? It is simply a thriller. There is nothing specially distinctive about it.'

'It seems they'd once thought of writing a book together,' Richard explained, 'and the title was to be *Taken As Red*, and also there are certain scenes in the book which she claims are descriptions of things that happened between the two of them. But perhaps I should add that Mrs Chilmark – Miss Acheson – claims that just those scenes – they're the love scenes, of course – were written by her and are completely fictitious.'

'But if you had never met Paul Clyro,' Raposo said, 'how were you to tell if he was Gavin Chilmark or not? He was hardly likely to admit he was.'

Richard took Clyro's passport out of his pocket.

'Mrs Clyro gave me this.'

Raposo opened it and thoughtfully compared it with the Chilmark passport, which he already had on the desk before him.

'These are not the same man,' he said.

'No.'

'So Mr Chilmark was not Mr Clyro.'

'So it seems.'

'You feel some doubts?'

'Well, as it happens, neither of those photographs is particularly like the man who's been living here under the name of Chilmark.'

'Ah. As he is at present, of course, it is impossible to tell that.' Raposo brought the tips of his well-manicured fingers together. 'Is it your opinion then that neither of these photographs is of him?'

'I simply don't know,' Richard said. 'For one thing, he was several years older than either of these two. Then he'd grown a beard. Also he'd had an illness which had partly paralysed the muscles on one side of his face. It had made his eyes different sizes and made one of them wink uncontrollably and dragged up one corner of his mouth. I've still not made up my mind whether he was the man I was looking for or not.'

'This man Clyro,' Raposo said, still contemplating the photographs with grave attention, 'can you tell me anything about him?'

'He was a scientist,' Richard said. 'A molecular biologist. He worked at a research station in the North of Scotland under a man called Wolsingham. I don't know if that name means anything to you here. To us it was notorious for a time. He was a virologist. He was also a spy and was just about to be arrested when he killed himself by taking a dose of potassium cyanide. Clyro wasn't implicated in any way. Officially, at least, he never came under suspicion. But he seems to have felt that everyone distrusted him – that, at least, is the story as I've heard it from a friend of his – and one day he disappeared, as I told you, leaving his wife to wonder, all this time, if he was alive or dead.'

'And you are in love with his wife,' Raposo observed. He did not appear to expect an answer. After a moment he went on, 'What you have told me at least simplifies one thing. It will be very easy to discover if our Mr Chilmark was your Mr Clyro, for if he was associated even in the most innocent way with the spy Wolsingham, then it is certain his fingerprints will be on record. He may not even have been aware of their being taken, but I can count, I think, on that having been done, and so we can have the prints of this man compared with them, and that will settle the matter beyond doubt. And if he was Clyro, there may be a political angle to this murder. But personally I am inclined to regard it as a crime of passion.'

'You think he was the man he said he was,' Richard said,

'and his wife tracked him down, perhaps through the book he wrote, much as Mrs Clyro thought she had, and came here and shot him in revenge for his desertion?'

Raposo hesitated. His melancholy eyes grew a degree sadder.

'Mr Hedon, what time was it this morning when Miss Acheson called for you at your hotel?' he asked.

'About half past nine.'

Raposo nodded. 'And our doctor has said he believes the murder probably took place between approximately nine o'clock and eleven o'clock this morning. It is not, of course, possible to be precise in this matter. But it is not impossible, you see, that Mr Chilmark was dead before Miss Acheson left the house.'

'Miss Acheson – that poor girl – you think *she* did it?' Richard exclaimed incredulously. 'Good God, she's almost demented with shock and grief.'

'Think,' Raposo said patiently. 'This man's wife comes suddenly to Madeira. She telephones that she must see him. What does he do? He tells this girl, who is madly in love with him, that she must not be here when his wife comes, she must go out for the day, take you for a drive, leave him and his wife together. What do you think, what do you really think, she would make of that? It appears to me she is a very passionate girl, very impulsive, very uncontrolled. I think she might well be so consumed with unbearable jealousy that when it came to driving away and leaving him to meet his wife, it was more than she could endure, and so she killed him. Tell me, what was her state when she arrived at the hotel to pick you up?'

'Not in the least like someone who'd just done a murder!'

'She was quite normal?'

'She seemed nervous at first. But that's explained by her knowing that Mrs Chilmark was coming to see her husband.'

'Well, I have still an open mind. I see that you do not like my theory.' Raposo gave an apologetic smile, as if he regretted having said something displeasing to Richard. 'I have another theory, but I am afraid you will like it even less.'

'What's that?' Richard asked.

'That no Mrs Chilmark came yesterday. That when we have checked, we will find no trace of her having come to Madeira. That she is a figment of the imagination of Miss Acheson and that what happened here was simply some fierce quarrel which resulted in the shooting. The grief and shock you have seen in Miss Acheson could still be quite sincere.'

'That theory isn't so very different from your other one. I mean, it doesn't explain her comparatively normal behaviour all today.'

'Perhaps not.'

'Have you found the weapon?'

'Not yet.'

'Anyway, how do you suppose a girl like Miss Acheson would get hold of a gun?'

Raposo gave a slight shrug and Richard realized that the man might not see it as important to delve very deeply into the inscrutable ways of foreigners. Where they came from, perhaps, for all he knew, they were able to buy guns over the counter, like pounds of sugar. And since the victim was a foreigner, it would really be most convenient all round if the murderer turned out to be a foreigner too.

'I know nothing yet of her background,' he said. 'She appears to be a well-bred girl, yet she lived openly with a man who was not her husband and shows no shame when she speaks of it. This I do not altogether understand. But, as I said, my mind is open.'

Richard hoped that it really was. Gillian as a murderess did not impress him. If it was not too difficult to imagine her in a rage that might almost be murderous, he could not see her going through the day that he and she had had together without betraying herself. He asked Raposo what was going to happen to her now and when he was told that that had not been decided yet, asked if he could see her again. But he was politely told that it would be best if he returned now to his hotel and remained there for the present. He need not worry about Miss Acheson, Raposo said, she would be well taken care of and would certainly not be left to spend the night alone in this house. Unsure whether this meant that she would be taken to a hotel, or to a police station, and deeply troubled, but not seeing just what he could do about it, Richard allowed himself to be sent off to Funchal in a taxi.

Dinner was long since over in his hotel. He ordered sandwiches and coffee to be sent to his room, and when he had finished them, went to the bar for a drink. He was just asking for a double whisky when he was tapped on the shoulder by Arthur Codsall.

'What's this I hear?' Codsall said.

'I don't know,' Richard said. 'What *have* you heard?'

'That there's been a murder, no less, out at our friend Chilmark's.'

Richard glanced round uneasily. He was tired and confused and did not want to find himself a centre of interest among the people in the bar, as the man who had been on the spot. But there were not many people there and dance music and the sound of scraping feet in the room next door appeared to have drowned Codsall's words. Richard carried his drink to a table by one of the big windows that overlooked the harbour, where Codsall, somewhat to Richard's annoyance, joined him.

At a table nearby the old couple who had sat near Richard in the dining-room were talking in their flat, penetrating voices.

'There's that young man who was next to us at dinner last night,' the woman said. 'He wasn't there tonight. I wonder where he went. He hasn't got himself a girl yet. You'd think he'd be dancing now, instead of just sitting there drinking with that odd-looking man.'

'That's a man I wouldn't like to get across,' her husband said. 'I shouldn't like to do that. I'm a very good judge of character, that's something I'm good at, and I know I shouldn't like to get across him.'

Richard tried to shut out the sound of their voices.

'How do you know anything about a murder?' he asked.

Codsall's nearly invisible eyebrows lifted in surprise. 'The place is buzzing with it.'

'Then why aren't those two over there talking about it?'

'Because they never listen to anything but the sound of their own voices. They'll be the last people to hear of it.'

It was a neat argument, if not particularly convincing.

'It isn't that you happened to stop off in Rua Ponte Nova on the way back from Porto Moniz and took a look inside Number Seven?' Richard asked.

'Good lord, why should I do that?'

'Because you're as interested as I am in whether Chilmark is Clyro.'

Codsall shook his head. 'I'm interested in you, Mr Hedon. I'm only interested in Chilmark because you're interested in him.'

'I don't believe you.'

Codsall gave a sigh, as if he found that the kind of remark to which it was not worth replying.

Richard went on. 'What have I ever done to get you security people interested in me?'

Again the pallid eyebrows were raised. 'Who said anything about security?'

'You did.'

'When?'

'Driving in from Vila do Bonfim.'

'You know, I can't think of a single thing I said to give you such a strange idea.'

Richard tried to think of one, and found, to his dismay, that he could not.

'Well, you let me think it,' he said.

'Isn't it your privilege to think what you like and mine to let you think it?'

'Who are you, then?'

Codsall smiled. 'You know, it wouldn't be any good my telling you, because you wouldn't believe me. By the way, have you been talking about me to the police here?'

'Not yet.'

'I wonder why not.'

'Because I knew, if I told them about your following Mrs Clyro around and following me out here, you'd simply deny everything I said, and it would just be my word against yours.'

'Good, I'm glad you realized that.'

'You would deny it, wouldn't you?'

'Certainly.'

At the table near them the woman remarked, 'Don't you think those two over there look as if they're hatching a plot of some kind? I wonder what they're up to. The way they whisper to one another, you can't hear a word they say.'

'It's something shady, I shouldn't wonder,' her husband said. 'A couple of crooks from Morocco, perhaps, hiding out here. Or revolutionaries.'

'Hijackers,' the woman suggested eagerly.

'Yes, something like that.'

'You know, I shouldn't be surprised if you're right,' she said. 'You're a great judge of character.'

'Yes, that's something I am.'

Codsall smiled broadly. 'Now that's something you didn't even think of, did you, Mr Hedon? Will you join me in a little hijacking tomorrow? Just an informal affair. No need to dress for it specially. Another thing you don't seem to have thought of is private enterprise. Why hasn't it struck you that I could be carrying out a private inquiry into the life of Mrs Clyro, to get evidence so that her husband can divorce her, and that that could be why I'm so interested in you?'

Richard frowned as he drank some of his whisky. 'Is that what you are – a private detective?'

Codsall laughed aloud. He took his wallet out of his pocket and extracted a card. It said, 'Arthur Codsall. Bureau of Investigation. Reliability. Discretion.' It gave an address in Soho. 'So now you know,' he said. 'Now suppose we leave it at that. Just remember that some women like Mrs Clyro, beautiful, living alone, are sometimes trailed by detectives for reasons that have nothing to do with politics. Now I'm off to bed. Good night. See you around in the morning, I expect.'

Richard muttered, 'Good night,' finished his drink slowly, then went to bed himself.

He did not see Codsall in the morning. He tried to do so, because he wanted to probe once more into how Codsall had obtained his information about the murder. For the hotel was not buzzing with it. So far the police had been very successful in keeping all knowledge of the event from the tourists. But when Richard asked the porter for Codsall's room number, he was told that he had gone. He had checked out in the early hours of the morning and left Madeira on the first flight to Lisbon.

Chapter Nine

Richard returned to his room and settled down on the balcony to stare sightlessly across the hibiscus and the palms at the sea. He began to think about Anne. He wished she were here, because then he could discuss with her what he ought to do.

Ought he to go to the police and tell them the curious story of Codsall? Would they believe it, if he did? Ought he to find out if they would let him see Gillian?

To try to see her seemed only human. She had said nothing, all the day before, to suggest that she had any close friends on the island. Gavin Chilmark had filled her whole life. So now she must feel quite dreadfully alone.

Then, ought he to try to get in touch by telephone with Hazel Clyro, to tell her what had happened to the man who she believed was her husband? Ought he to find out if the police would let him fly home to see her and tell her, face to face, about the murder?

Since Anne was not there, he talked to her in imagination, as he often did, putting these problems to her, and if he had not the help of her actual answers, at least his mind became a little clearer as he frowned and thought and occasionally spoke a few words aloud and gesticulated with one hand, as if doing that would help to explain the situation to her across all the intervening miles of Atlantic Ocean.

He seldom realized how much he needed Anne until she was out of reach. Then he began to feel as if a part of his own brain, on which he could normally rely, had been lopped away, and as if his mind were having to stumble along in a one-legged sort of way, able to take in only a fraction of what he needed if he were to proceed in a wise and balanced manner.

'Look, Anne,' he said to her inside his head, 'I know I'm a hopeless fool at times, but I do find it difficult to swallow the coincidence that *two* men who wanted to write a book called *Taken As Red* should happen to desert their wives about the same time, and that both their wives should get on to them about the same time too. And yet if it's true that a woman came here yesterday called Margaret Chilmark, I don't see how she can be Hazel Clyro. Unless – unless – ' Richard's mind suddenly began to whir like a machine beginning to get out of control. It was a horrible feeling. He wanted to stop it, but could not find the switch that would turn it off. ' – unless she and Clyro were in the Wolsingham business up to their necks and both had false passports and were ready to bolt when he killed himself. And when that happened, for some reason, it wasn't necessary for them to go, so they stayed, until one day Clyro wanted out – out of the spying business and out of his marriage. Yet Hazel told me – she *told* me and I absolutely believed her – that her approach to politics was at the jumble sale level and that she wanted people to see each other just as people and not always be on one side or other of some fence ... '

The telephone rang.

He went into his room and answered it. Mr Raposo, he was told, was in the hotel and would like a quiet word with him. Richard asked where the *Senhor Chefe* would like the quiet word. It was suggested that Richard's room would be as good a place as any.

Raposo appeared a minute or two later. He looked as well-groomed and as coolly unaffected by the heat of midday as he had the evening before. But when he took off the dark glasses that he had been wearing, Richard saw that there were shadows under his eyes, as if he had not had much time for sleep. They went out to the balcony and sat down there, Raposo taking out cigarettes, and when Richard refused one, lighting one himself and sitting quietly smoking for a moment before he spoke.

Then he said, 'I have come to tell you that if you wish to return home, there is no reason why you should not do so. I thought it might also be of interest to you to know that we have traced Mrs Chilmark.'

Because of his own thoughts of a few minutes before, a chill spread through Richard.

'You've found her?'

'No, that will be for your police to do,' Raposo answered. 'What I mean is, we have traced her movements in Madeira. Also, we have a description of her and the number of her passport. It will not be difficult for your police to find her. I feel sure of that.'

'That description of her – what's she like?' Richard asked, trying to keep his voice casual.

'Of medium height and dark-haired. She was wearing a flowered trouser suit, a large shady hat, and dark spectacles, so that it was impossible to tell the colour of her eyes. And she arrived with one small suitcase and carried a large red plastic handbag.'

'That means that except for her height and the colour of her hair, you don't know much about her,' Richard said, but he felt an immense relief.

It was slightly damped when Raposo said, 'That is true, but some ladies frequently change the colour of their hair. However – ,' he smiled ' – you should remember that she passed through several passport controls, and if the colour of her hair was different from that stated in her passport, a question might have been asked. Further, the manageress in the hotel where she stayed in Funchal believes she was described in the passport as dark-haired.'

'Where did she stay in Funchal?' Richard asked.

'At the Vila Angela. It is a small hotel not far from here. She stayed there only for one night. The night before last. She came to Madeira on the late plane that evening and asked one of the taxi-drivers to take her to a not too expensive hotel. As soon as she got there she said that she wanted to make a telephone call and asked the manageress to help her, as she could not speak Portuguese. She wanted the manageress to look up the number of Mr Gavin Chilmark in the directory and to put the call through to him, then as soon as there was an answer, to hand the telephone over. The manageress did this. The answer came in a woman's voice, the manageress gave Mrs Chilmark the telephone and did not listen to the call. But she did hear Mrs Chilmark say, 'Tell him it's Margaret.'

'That corroborates what Miss Acheson told you,' Richard said.

'Perfectly,' Raposo agreed.

'What else do you know about this woman?'

'Well, she appears to have made no attempt to conceal her

movements,' Raposo answered. 'In the morning she asked for an early breakfast, paid her bill and called a taxi. In the hotel it was thought that she was leaving for the airport, but we have found the driver of the taxi she took and he says she asked to be taken in the opposite direction, to Vila do Bonfim. She was leaving on the second plane of the morning, she said, and wanted to see a little of the island before she left, besides, she had a visit to make. She directed him to 7 Rua Ponte Nova, and when they reached it, told him to wait for her. As she went up the path to the house, a man appeared in the doorway, a tall, bearded man who was certainly Mr Chilmark. The driver did not hear their greeting, but saw them go into the house together. This was about half past nine. After about two minutes the woman came out again. By then a crowd of children had collected round the car. When they saw Mrs Chilmark, they mobbed her, as you may have seen them do, demanding *escudos*. One of them tried to put his hand into her red plastic handbag and she seems to have lost her head and screamed at him and hit him. If the taxi-driver had not interfered, he thinks, she might have found herself in trouble, but he chased the children away and drove off.'

Raposo looked at Richard gravely through a haze of cigarette smoke.

'He thought she was surprisingly upset by the incident with the children,' he said. 'He could see that she was very white and kept on having attacks of trembling all the way to the airport. We, of course, know it was not the incident with the children that had upset her. She had just committed a murder. The gun with which she did it was probably in that big red handbag. She caught the mid-morning plane for Lisbon and by the time you and Miss Acheson discovered Mr Chilmark's body, was probably already in London.'

Richard was silent for a moment, marvelling at the breadth of the trail that the woman had left behind her.

'What about the sound of the shot?' he asked. 'Didn't the driver or the children hear anything?'

Raposo gave a dry little laugh. 'Oh yes, they heard it. But you know, here in Madeira we have a way of letting off rockets on fête days. It is unusual to let them off so early in the morning, it is usually in the evenings, but still, it could have been someone experimenting, or a child who had got hold of one and wanted to make it go bang. That, I should say, would have seemed a likelier explanation than that the lady who had come there so openly should simply have gone into the house, shot the man who lived there, and come out again with the gun in her red bag. Who would have thought of such a thing?'

'Anyway, Miss Acheson is completely exonerated,' Richard said. 'If the driver saw Chilmark alive at half past nine, which is the time she picked me up here, she couldn't have had anything to do with his murder. You can't go on holding her.'

'But we are not *holding* her, Mr Hedon!' Raposo exclaimed. 'She spent the night in a hotel in Funchal. We took her there for her own comfort. It would not have been good for her to stay alone in that house, with the neighbours there already hostile to her because of what they consider her immorality. But she is free to leave at any time she chooses. Only we have asked her to remain in Madeira for the present, in case further problems should arise.'

'Can I go and see her?'

'Of course, of course!' Raposo got to his feet. 'She is in bad need of help. Her condition is tragic. Last night she was in a state of hopeless hysteria. She was given a sedative, but I do not know how much it helped. Has she any family in England, do you know?'

'Two aunts, I believe,' Richard answered.

'Perhaps they should be sent for.'

'From what she told me about them, I rather think not.'

'But she is quite alone, and such a young girl.'

'I'll see what I can do,' Richard said.

'Good, I am glad of that. In this permissive society that we hear so much about, the young must very often find themselves out of their depths.'

'Don't we all, at some time?'

'Yes, perhaps.'

'I feel out of mine now.'

'Do you, Mr Hedon? Why?'

'This is my first brush with murder. The boldness, the openness of it completely bewilder me. For it must have been premeditated, mustn't it? She brought the gun with her.' He stood up too. 'Where is this hotel Miss Acheson's in?'

'It is the Casa do Parque.' Raposo gave him instructions how to find it, and left him.

Since the Casa do Parque was only a few hundred yards from his own hotel, Richard walked to it along the shadeless, baking pavement that edged the narrow road. He had forgotten to put on his dark glasses, and the glare of the sunshine dazzled him. It was very hot. He saw a man, lounging by one of the inevitable waiting taxis, spit luxuriously on to the cobbles. He looked pleased with the result and spat again. The spittle dried in an instant. A lizard flicked across the pavement, with a lean cat chasing it. Richard turned in at the entrance of the Casa do Parque and asked for Miss Acheson.

A small, dark, dumpy maid took him to Gillian's room. The maid kept smiling at him sympathetically to show that she was delighted that someone was coming to visit the poor bereaved girl upstairs, and Richard could only smile back to show that he appreciated this interest. The maid tapped on a door and spoke gently. An apathetic voice answered and Richard opened the door.

Gillian, wearing a plain white cotton dress that brought out all her childishness, was lying on the bed. Her eyes were dry, but were red from recent crying. Her face was puffy and her hair hung around it in a dishevelled mass.

She looked at Richard indifferently and said, 'What d'you want?'

'To see if I can help in any way,' he said.

'How can anyone help?'

'Well, may I come in?'

She gave a vague nod and Richard gave another smile to the waiting maid and closed the door on her. The room was small and plain, without a balcony and with only a small glimpse of the sea between two tall buildings. There was one armchair in the room. Richard dropped into it.

'You know the police don't suspect you any more, I suppose,' he said.

'What does it matter if they do or not?' she asked.

'Well, you are free to go, for one thing.'

'Where should I go?'

'That's something I thought we might talk about.'

'What's it got to do with you?'

'Absolutely nothing, of course. But I don't see why that means we shouldn't talk about it.'

She raised herself on an elbow and looked at him with the first trace of interest that she had shown.

'You aren't starting to feel responsible for me, are you?' she said. 'People sometimes do, but it never does them any good.'

'Hasn't it sometimes done you some good?'

'I don't think so. I've got to go my own way. I've got to think things out for myself. Nobody can help me.'

'That's a rather terrible statement.'

'I suppose I'm a terrible person. I've often thought I must be.'

'Shall I go away, then?'

'If you want to.'

'I don't want to at all.'

'Then stay. It's – it's nice of you to come. I'm not really ungrateful.' She did not smile, but there was a little more warmth in her voice. 'You do understand, don't you, I've got to think things out carefully and not do anything stupid? It would be very easy just now for me to rush back home to my aunts. They'd forgive me at once and welcome me back with open arms and kill the fatted sherry bottle in my honour. But it would be so unfair on them, because I'd only have to leave them all over again . . . ' She gave a deep sigh and lay back on the pillows.

After a moment she raised herself again and looked curiously at Richard.

'What are you thinking about?' she asked.

'Lunch,' he answered.

'Well, go, if you want to.'

'I was thinking you probably need lunch as much as I do.'

'Oh, I'm not hungry,' she said. 'I couldn't eat anything.'

'I should think you could, if you tried, and food can be very consoling.' He had seen the day before that normally she had an excellent appetite and he thought that someone should make sure that she had something to eat today. 'We could go into the country again, or somewhere in Funchal.'

He saw indecision on her face.

'But I can't go out like this,' she said. 'Everyone can see I've been crying. I couldn't stand being stared at.'

'Put on some dark glasses.'

'No, I really couldn't. It's very kind of you, but I'd feel too awful.'

Richard was silent again.

After a moment, she added, 'Well, I suppose I *could* . . .'

'Of course you could,' he said. 'Come along. Just wash your face first and do your hair.'

She made a sound that was almost a small laugh. 'You sound just like a nannie. I had a nannie once. I loved her. You know, I'm not sure that isn't what I need now, a nannie with a nice motherly bosom to shed my tears on.'

'My bosom isn't motherly,' Richard said; 'but it's had tears shed on it before now. So come along.'

She swung her legs down from the bed.

'All right, wait for me downstairs.'

A few minutes later, when she came down after him, her hair had been brushed and hung straight and smooth down her back, she had on big dark glasses that hid most of the signs of her tears, and she had a touch of lipstick on her mouth, which made it look less swollen. But there was an unnatural stiffness about her walk, as if it took an effort to make herself keep moving.

'Where shall we go?' Richard asked. 'I was wondering if my hotel might not be the best place. It's big and anonymous. No one will take any notice of you there, if that's how you want it.'

'All right, let's go there.'

He thought that she would have said that it was all right, whatever he had suggested. She took his arm and they walked across the cobbled pavement together.

But Richard found that he had been wrong in thinking that Gillian would not be noticed in the big, busy dining-room of his hotel. As soon as they sat down at his usual table, the couple at the next table started talking about them.

'Well, at last he's got himself a girl,' the woman said with her usual appalling distinctness. 'I wonder where he picked her up. Must have worked fast, to bring her here to lunch. Looks half his age. That's the type he is, I suppose.'

'I can't stand those big black goggles they wear nowadays,' the man said. 'Makes them all look like ghouls.'

'Wearing them indoors too,' the woman said. 'Just a ridiculous affectation.'

Richard grinned encouragingly at Gillian. 'Well, ghoul, what do you want to eat?'

To his dismay, he saw that her jaw was trembling.

'I'm sorry, Richard, but honestly I don't think I'm going to be able to eat anything at all.'

'You are, and I'll just go ahead and choose it for you. The *hors d'œuvres* are good here, and we could try the fish dish, I should think, whatever it is. And some wine – *rosé* of some sort, perhaps. I don't know one from another, so we'll let the waiter advise us. And if those two characters over there go on talking about us, just take no notice, unless they amuse you. I admit they do me. They've brightened up my stay here considerably.'

Gillian put her elbows on the table and rested her head on her hands.

'Richard, why haven't you got married?' she asked.

He was startled. 'Me?'

'You could make a woman so happy,' she said. 'You're really kind. Not just good-natured when it suits you, and neglectful or downright vicious when it doesn't. You really seem to care about people. That's what matters if you're going to live with a person, besides being attractive and sexually exciting and so on, of course. And you've got to need kindness yourself too, or things get lopsided. Gavin was wonderfully kind. But Margaret never had any use for that side of him, so it got sort of tied up in knots till he found me to look after. I think that's mostly why he left her. Of course, I've thought about that a lot – why he walked out. But why haven't you married? Is it because of this Clyro woman?'

'Not really,' Richard said. 'Not if you want the truth. The fact is, I've only known her for a short time. So it goes a long way farther back than that.'

122

'Is it somebody else, then?'

'It was, for a long time.'

'Why didn't she want you? She must be awfully stupid.'

'No, she isn't stupid. She just happens to be in love with somebody else.'

'Is she married to him?'

He hesitated. 'No.'

She shook her head sorrowfully. 'It all sounds awfully sad and muddled up. I'm sure you could do something about it if you wanted to. But you don't even want to talk about it, do you?'

'Not much.' There was an interlude while he gave their order to a waiter. 'Let's talk about you, Gillian. About what you're going to do.'

'But I told you, I don't know. I suppose I'll look for a job, but I don't know what. I've never been trained for anything. Perhaps I could work in a shop or something.'

'If you've got some money to live on, you could afford to take a training of some kind.'

'I've lots of money.' It sounded about as forlorn as such a statement could. 'There's my own, which isn't much, but Gavin made a will, leaving everything he had to me, and that's quite a lot now. And Margaret isn't going to be able to contest that will, as she killed him. Can you understand her doing it, Richard? Can you understand hating a person so much, only for leaving you, that two years afterwards you'll chase him as far as this, just for the sake of a couple of minutes' talk with him and the chance to kill him?'

'No, but I don't think I can see myself murdering anybody, at least not cold-bloodedly, though perhaps there are circumstances . . . ' He paused. Something that Gillian had said held his attention. 'Perhaps that wasn't her only reason for doing it. Perhaps there was some good solid reason why she wanted him dead.'

'Well, if it was his money, she shouldn't have left such an obvious trail, should she?'

'Perhaps she didn't realize it was an obvious trail.'

'Then she's a bit dim-witted.'

'I wonder . . . '

The *hors d'œuvres* trolley was wheeled up to them and Gillian started choosing things from it. She did it absent-mindedly and from the amount with which she let her plate be heaped, it seemed that she had forgotten that she did not think that she could eat anything. By the time that the waiter left them she seemed also to have forgotten what they had been talking about and began to eat with all the signs of a healthy hunger.

After that she polished off her fish with energy, then thought that she would like one of the squashy-looking cakes on another trolley that was wheeled up to them for inspection.

It was over coffee afterwards that Richard said to her, 'I think I'm going home tomorrow, if I can get a booking on a plane. But I'm going to give you my address, then if you come to London you can get in touch with me, if you want to. If there's any way I can help you, I will.'

He tore a page out of his diary, wrote his address and telephone number on it and gave it to her. She put it away in her handbag.

'Would it really not be a nuisance if I turned up sometime?' she asked.

He thought that it very well might be, but that there were some nuisances that had to be borne.

'Of course not,' he said.

'I said you were kind.' She was silent for a moment, then went on, 'You know what you said about Margaret having a more solid reason for killing Gavin than just hatred . . . '

'Yes?'

'What did you mean?'

'Nothing specific. I just wondered if perhaps she had, say, some reason to be afraid of him.'

'No one could have been afraid of him.'

'Suppose he had some hold over her, knew something about her.'

'He'd never have used it. All he wanted was to forget her.'

'She may not have known that.'

Gillian looked dubious and said, 'I suppose that's possible, but all the same . . . ' She shook her head.

'But you don't really know much about his past, do you?'

124

Richard said. 'He was a journalist, and he was unhappily married, that's all you've told me about him. Do you really know much more?'

'Not really, no. We always had so much else to talk about.'

'You wouldn't know for sure, for instance, if sometime he'd got himself involved with the kind of people who might be dangerous. As a journalist he may have come across some curious things. And that woman, Margaret, left such a broad trail that I can't help wondering *was* she Margaret, or was she someone else, deliberately laying that trail to mislead us.'

'Oh!' Gillian exclaimed. 'I hadn't thought of that.' She chewed her thumb, then after some deep thought shook her head again. 'No, it must have been Margaret, because she spoke to Gavin on the telephone, and he'd have known her voice, wouldn't he?'

'I suppose he would.'

'He'd no doubts himself about who it was.'

'Well, there are other possibilities.'

They talked for a little longer, then Gillian said that she must go.

Richard walked back to her hotel with her, then went on into the town to see if he could make a booking on a flight back to London next day. He found no difficulty in doing this. Returning to his hotel, he had another swim, then lay in the sun until it began to dip behind the hills on the far side of the bay.

With the coming of twilight, he began to imagine that he could smell the pungent scent of the datura in the little garden of the house in Vila do Bonfim, and the memory of the scene that he and Gillian had found there returned to him with harrowing clarity. He remembered Gillian's wailing, and the obscene flies circling drowsily about the room. Richard had met Gavin Chilmark only once, but he had liked him, and he had an unnerving feeling of having brought disaster to him. Of course, that was absurd. All the same, for the rest of the evening, he was haunted by a morbid sense of guilt, as if somehow it were he who had set in motion the events that had led up to the murder.

Next day it was about six o'clock when his plane landed at

Heathrow. The long spell of fine weather had broken and a thin, chill rain greeted him, whipped into his face as he walked towards the airport bus by a gusty little wind. Other passengers in the bus, returning from Madeira or the sunshine of Portugal, complained sadly. This was summer, they said. It didn't take you long to realize you'd got home, did it? At the Cromwell Road terminal, Richard took a taxi and arrived at the house in St John's Wood soon after eight o'clock.

As he let himself in at the door, he heard Bernard and Harriet talking in the dining-room, and the rich smell of steak and kidney pie drifted out of it. It was a heartening smell for someone who had had nothing to eat all day but aeroplane meals and who was feeling chilled to the marrow by the abrupt change of climate.

Richard put his head in at the door and said, 'Hallo – anything left for me?'

They both exclaimed, 'Richard!' and Harriet, getting quickly to her feet and picking up the pie, said, 'I'll pop it back in the oven for a little – it probably isn't as hot as it might be. Whatever brought you back so soon?'

'I had reasons. I'll tell you about them presently. Now I'll go upstairs and wash.'

'Don't be too long,' Harriet said. 'I don't want the pie to dry up.'

'Nor do I,' Richard said.

He went upstairs to his flat.

As soon as he had closed the door behind him, he put down his suitcase and went straight to the telephone. He dialled Hazel's number. There was no reply. He let the telephone ring at least a dozen times before he put it down again. He stood frowning at it. For a moment he felt an inclination to skip the steak and kidney pie, get out his car and drive over to her flat, in case, for some reason, she had got into a mood of not answering the telephone. But actually it was slightly more likely that he had dialled the wrong number. He tried again, paying extra special attention to where he put his finger. Again he heard the telephone ringing, unanswered.

He took off his coat and tie, went into the bathroom and washed, put on a warm sweater instead of his jacket, brushed his hair and was about to go downstairs to join Bernard and Harriet when he had another idea. He would telephone the Ottershaws. Hazel might be with them. Hunting up their number in the directory, he dialled and was almost immediately answered by Jerome.

'Richard!' he said heartily. 'We thought you were in Madeira. How did the hunt for Clyro go? No luck, I imagine. Did you have a good time?'

'Not exactly,' Richard said. 'I'll tell you all about it another time. Jerome – '

'What about tomorrow?' Jerome bore him down. 'Lunch – what about having lunch with me tomorrow? At the Europa again, unless you've got a better idea.'

'I don't think I can manage tomorrow,' Richard answered. 'I've a lot to catch up on. What I rang up about, Jerome, was to ask if by any chance Hazel's with you this evening?'

'No,' Jerome said, 'not this evening. Why? Did she say she might be?'

'No, it was just an idea of mine. I rather badly want to get in touch with her.'

'Ah, to report on Clyro. He *wasn't* Clyro, was he, Richard?'

'Probably not.'

'What d'you mean, probably? Don't you know?'

'There's an element of uncertainty in the situation. I suppose you've no idea where Hazel might be.'

'God knows, cinema, theatre, anywhere. But I'll ask Jeannie if she knows. Hazel may have mentioned it in one of those long chats the girls keep having on the telephone. Jeannie – '

Richard heard him calling out the question to Jeannie.

A moment later Jeannie's deep voice spoke to him. 'Richard! You're looking for Hazel? I'm sorry, I haven't heard anything from her for several days. Is it urgent?'

'In a way. Never mind. I'll try ringing her up again later in the evening.'

'I'm sorry we can't help. But do tell us what happened in Madeira. Did you find Paul?'

'Actually I'm not sure, but I expect I'll know soon,' Richard answered. The press, he thought, would see to it that they all did if the dead man had been Paul Clyro. The Wolsingham story would be revived. The murder would be important news for a few days. Meanwhile, knowing that he would shortly have to tell the whole story of what had happened in Madeira to Bernard and Harriet, Richard did not feel inclined to tell it now. 'I'll ring up again when I do know for certain.'

'You sound very mysterious,' Jeannie said.

'Just tired. Not as clear in the head as I might be. Good night, Jeannie. Sorry to have bothered you.'

Richard put the telephone down and went downstairs to the steak and kidney pie.

Over it he told Bernard and Harriet the story of the murder of Gavin Chilmark. He tried to keep it short and simple, saying no more than he had to about Gillian, almost omitting Arthur Codsall, and being brief and abrupt about the shock of finding the dead body. All the same, there seemed to be a great deal to say, and Harriet had removed his empty plate and replaced it with one of queen of puddings before he came to the end. Bernard had listened to it with silent attention, but Harriet had kept interrupting with questions, which had often muddled Richard and made him forget what he had been about to say. What he had told Jeannie, that he was tired and that his head was not as clear as it might be, was perfectly true.

In the end Bernard summed up for him. 'So on the whole you're inclined to think this man Chilmark wasn't Clyro, for the simple reason that there appears to be a Mrs Chilmark, who you don't think could be Hazel Clyro.'

'That's it, more or less,' Richard agreed, keeping his doubts to himself.

'I feel sorry for that girl, Gillian,' Harriet said. 'I wonder what will become of her.'

'Incidentally, while you've been gone,' Bernard said, 'I dug up something that may interest you. It was in my files. I'll go and get it.'

Bernard's files were an institution in the house, occupying most of the space in the room that was called his study. On what system he selected items for inclusion in them, or how his index functioned, no one but himself had ever fathomed, but the grey steel drawers contained, besides letters and notes, an immense collection of newspaper clippings on subjects that had caught Bernard's interest for a time. Together with his formidable memory, they made him almost invincible in any argument, or would have done so if he had been in the way of getting involved in disputes. His normal habit was to sidle tactfully away if ever one started.

Ambling out of the dining-room now, he returned in a minute or two with a clipping that he handed to Richard.

It was a photograph of Wolsingham. The caption under it merely stated that the distinguished scientist had been found dead in his laboratory and that the cause of death was believed to be a dose of potassium cyanide. At the time when it had been printed, the story of his spying could not have been released yet.

Richard stared at it with a kind of disbelief. He saw a longish face with a high, narrow forehead and close-cropped hair, a taut, intense face, with an expression both forceful and bitter, a familiar face, which Richard had seen, he had no doubt of it, only two days ago in the passport of Gavin Chilmark.

But Wolsingham had been dead for three years.

Then how had he turned into Gavin Chilmark and been resurrected in Vila do Bonfim?

Chapter Ten

At eleven-thirty that evening Richard again tried to telephone Hazel. Again there was no response.

He did not sleep much that night. Wolsingham was on his mind and would not remove himself. Those powerful, nervous features haunted Richard even through the few short snatches of sleep that he achieved, the face that he saw in them becoming monstrous and inhuman. Which might be the truth about the man, Richard thought, during one of his long stretches of wakefulness. Not merely because of his beliefs, with which you might deeply disagree, but which a large proportion of the human race appeared to find perfectly acceptable, but because there was something monstrous and inhuman about living in daily contact with a small group of people and betraying their trust in you with every breath you drew.

One of the people whom Wolsingham had most deeply betrayed was Paul Clyro. And Clyro now lay dead in some mortuary in Madeira, murdered by Wolsingham's wife. The wife whom no one had known existed.

For of course it had not been Wolsingham who had been living in Madeira, in spite of that photograph in the Chilmark passport. There had never been any doubt that Wolsingham had died by his own hand of poison taken in his laboratory three years ago. For if death from a dose of potassium does not leave a man looking at his best, it does not so disguise him that there can be any doubt as to his identity.

No, Wolsingham had died, and Clyro, who had found the body, had also found the forged passport, with which Wolsingham must have been intending to escape behind the Iron Curtain. But apparently he had left it too late, and so had killed himself, sooner than face trial and years of imprisonment. And Clyro, for reasons best known to himself, had kept that passport hidden away until he too had wanted to disappear. Then it had come in very handy. For there had been enough superficial resemblance between the two men that with a new hair-cut, Clyro had been able to pass for the man called Chilmark.

But Clyro had not disappeared behind any Iron Curtain. He had merely gone away to a sunny island in the Atlantic, where he had settled down to a beachcombing existence, picking up a charming girl who adored him and writing a successful thriller. And to help his disguise, he had kept his hair cut like Wolsingham's, while growing a beard. And nature had helped him further in the discarding of his old identity by afflicting him with Bell's palsy. Even Gillian Acheson, seeing him daily, had never suspected that the photograph in the passport, which she must have seen, was not of him.

Which left the problems, as before, of why Clyro had suddenly deserted Hazel, to whom everyone appeared to believe he had been happily married, and of where Margaret Chilmark fitted in.

Margaret . . .

The voice that had spoken to Gillian on the telephone had said, 'Tell him it's Margaret.' And Clyro had always spoken to Gillian of his wife as Margaret, an odd thing to have done, when you came to think of it. It was as if he had had to remind himself constantly that he was Chilmark, not Clyro, and since Margaret was the name of Chilmark's wife, or rather, Wolsingham's, had always used that name. At the same time, it was as if he were somehow denying the existence of Hazel, blotting her out of his life and his mind.

Was it because he had known the identity of Margaret that he had died? Having recklessly drawn attention to himself by writing under the name of Chilmark, had he invited death?

The long hours passed until daylight began to show dimly at the window.

About six o'clock Richard got up, had a bath and made some coffee. At seven-thirty he again dialled Hazel's number. She would be awake by now, he thought, but would not yet have left for work. She was bound to answer.

She did not.

He let the ringing go on and on, feeling that he had only to wait a moment more to hear her voice. When nothing happened, he began to feel a futile exasperation with the telephone service for failing him so badly. Why couldn't he get through to her? At last he put the instrument down and started to dress in a hurry.

He went downstairs quietly. He could hear Harriet in the kitchen and did not want to draw her attention to him. He got his car out of the garage. Driving off, he was in the grip of a bewildered dread. Even if Hazel had been out the evening before, surely she ought to have been at home this morning. It was a weekday. She ought to have been getting ready to go to work. There was something wrong, or at least something very strange, about her not answering the telephone.

He drove fast. The traffic was not yet heavy and he reached the flat in Kentish Town in under fifteen minutes. He got quickly out of the car, strode in at the gate of the small, dingy square of garden in front of the house, and pressed an impatient finger on the doorbell.

Like the telephone, it remained unanswered.

So she had spent the night with a friend perhaps. Wasn't that obviously what had happened? There was no reason for anxiety. For jealousy, possibly. Richard experienced a sudden painful stab of it, and remembered Codsall and his hint that it was at the orders of a jealous wife that he had been following Hazel. The fact that Richard had never noticed any sign of another man in her life did not mean, with someone as self-contained as Hazel, that she was not seeing one every day.

But then Richard noticed certain disturbing things, and the sense of dread came sharply back. First, there were two milk-bottles on the doorstep. Then the curtains of the living-room were drawn and through the chink at the top of them he could see the yellow glow of electric light.

The milk-bottles were really nothing much to worry about. Though it was highly unlikely that Hazel drank milk at the rate of two pints a day and that they had both been delivered that morning, she could easily have forgotten, if she had suddenly decided to go away for a day or two, to leave a note for the milkman, cancelling her regular order. But why had that light been left on all night? Was that forgetfulness too?

Richard stepped back from the door and looked the house over.

There were only two floors, Hazel's flat on the ground floor and another flat above. The windows of the upper flat were draped in white net, but Richard could see a shadow behind one of them. Someone up there was looking down at him. The doors of both flats were side by side. Richard rang the bell of the upper one.

Immediately he heard the sound of slippers coming slapping down the stairs inside. A small woman in a flowered dressing-gown, with her grey hair on pink plastic rollers, peered out at him shortsightedly, gave a little gasp of dismay and clutched her dressing-gown closer about her.

'Oh, I beg your pardon, I thought you were the milkman,' she said in a dry little voice. If he had been the milkman, Richard realized, there would have been no apology for the dressing-gown. 'I was looking out for him. I thought he might be worrying about those bottles of hers – whether to leave any more, I mean, or not. I don't rightly know what to do about it myself. That first pint must have gone sour by now, even though the weather hasn't been as hot as it was, and if she's gone away and forgotten to tell him, it's sheer waste to go on. But I don't like to interfere, with her being such a one for keeping you at arm's length.'

'Then the milkman hasn't been round this morning,' Richard said.

'Not yet, he hasn't. But what's that to you?' she asked. 'You didn't come to talk about the milk, did you? What was it you want, dear?'

'I'm trying very hard to get in touch with Mrs Clyro,' he said. 'I'm sorry to have troubled you, but it's urgent that I should. I tried telephoning her last night and again this morning, and couldn't get any answer, so I came round, hoping I'd catch her before she set off for her work. But she doesn't answer the doorbell either. So I thought I'd ask you if you happened to know if she's gone away.'

'Well, except for the milk, I don't know anything,' she answered. 'But she's very quiet, it isn't often I hear her moving about, or the radio even. So if she was away for a night or two, I wouldn't notice. I did notice the milk-bottle stood on the doorstep all Sunday, but she took it in in the evening, then she's left Monday's and Tuesday's there, which looks as if she's gone away, but I couldn't tell you where or what to do, because I've got careful about having my head snapped off for interfering where I wasn't wanted.'

'I suppose she doesn't leave a key with you if she goes away,' Richard said.

'Not her!' the little woman snapped. 'That's what I do myself when I go to my sister's, I leave a key with Mrs Selby at Number Two, in case of accidents, because you never know, do you, with water, gas and all? I remember I was away once in the winter and I came back to a flood, a real flood, pouring down the stairs and out under this door, from a burst pipe in the roof, all because I'd never thought to leave the key with anyone. So now I always take it to Mrs Selby and say, "Go in and take a look round, dear, when you've got the time, I won't think it's nosiness." But of course I'd leave it with Mrs Clyro, that being more sensible, her living just downstairs, if she hadn't made it clear she can get along without her neighbours. Sometimes I feel sorry for her, living all alone like she does, with just an odd visitor now and then, but if you ask me, it's her own fault, only snubbing you if you make a friendly overture. If I was to say to her, "Why don't you leave a key with me, dear, when you go away, because after all there could be a fire, couldn't there?" she'd only think it was nosiness, me planning to get inside and look around. So I've given up bothering about her. But I don't like to think of that milk going to waste. What d'you think I ought to do about it?'

'I think I should leave it there for the present,' Richard said.

'But what shall I tell the milkman, if he asks?'

'Whatever you think best. Talk it over with him.' The problem was beyond Richard just then. 'Anyway, I'm sorry to have troubled you. Good morning.'

'Cheerio,' she said lugubriously. The wrinkled little face withdrew. The door closed.

Richard retreated to the gate.

But he paused there and turned to look again at the window with the drawn curtains. That light inside hadn't been imagination, had it? No, he could see it, making a pale yellow stain on the daylight.

At the window above a blurred form appeared once more behind the net curtain. His movements were being observed by the woman.

All the same, he made up his mind that he could not leave without knowing more about why that light had been left on in the living-room. Taking the path that led along the side of the small, semi-detached house, past dustbins and a coal-bunker, he went round to the yard at the back and took a look at the windows there.

One of the windows was Hazel's bedroom. Its curtains were not drawn. Going close to it, Richard peered in and saw that the bed was made and covered by a bedspread, that drawers and cupboards were closed, and that there was no clothing lying about. There was, indeed, an almost strange emptiness about the room. There were no brush and comb, no hand-mirror, no creams or bottles on the dressing-table. Only a small vase with a single faded rose in it on the bedside table prevented it looking like a hotel room, waiting for an occupant.

The window next to the bedroom was that of the bathroom. It had frosted glass and he could not see in. But next to the bathroom was the kitchen. He had been in it once, a minute cupboard of a place, with an old-fashioned sink with a wooden draining-board under the window, some shelves on one wall with tins and packets jammed together along them, a small refrigerator, and a stained, battered-looking gas stove of a pattern that was at least twenty years old. As the other rooms in the flat did, it showed Hazel as utterly indifferent to her surroundings. Also, like the bedroom, it had an unused look, a look of having been deserted. The wood of the draining-board was so dry that it was evident that no one had used the sink for a day or two. So was a nearly worn-out washing-up mop stuck in a jam-jar on the windowsill.

Richard stood thinking, doing a little calculating.

Hazel had left her milk-bottle on the doorstep for most of Sunday, but had fetched it in in the evening. That looked as if she had gone away on Saturday, returning towards evening on the following day. But she had not taken in Monday's or Tuesday's milk. So she must have come home only for a brief time, going out again almost immediately.

Why? And where?

Her reason for coming home might simply have been to pick up some extra clothes. Suppose on the Saturday or the Sunday she had come to some decision that had meant that she must stay away for longer than she had intended, or even go away for good, she would of course need more clothes than she had taken for the one night.

Suppose she had got married and gone away on a honeymoon . . .

No, not if she believed Chilmark was Clyro, thought Richard. He must keep his head. But the trouble was, he really knew dreadfully little about her. She had always seemed to like being with him, but had never taken him into her confidence. Almost certainly there was some quite simple explanation of what she had done. So why was he worrying?

The answer was that she had been expecting news from him

135

in Madeira. That made it a strange time for her to go away.

Coming abruptly to a decision, Richard stooped, picked up a stone that was lying at his feet in the untidy back yard and smashed one of the panes in the kitchen window with it.

His heart beat uncomfortably fast as he thrust an arm through the jagged hole that he had made and reached for the latch. He was not accustomed to housebreaking. He felt somewhat frightened at what he had done. But he wasted no time in opening the window, then getting one knee up on to the windowsill and hauling himself inside.

Scrambling across the sink and dropping to the floor, he stood still for an instant, listening. The flat was silent. It seemed that there was no one there to be alarmed by the sounds of his noisy entry. Opening the kitchen door, he went along the narrow passage and into the living-room.

Afterwards, in his memories of that first moment in the room with the drawn curtains and the ceiling light shining, he was almost ready to swear that before anything else, he had noticed the heavy scent of datura. Of course that was nonsense. Daturas do not grow in Kentish Town. His senses were confused. It was something else that he smelled, far more dreadful, which just happened to be linked in his mind with the scent of datura. It was the smell of death.

She was sprawling in a chair, as Gavin Chilmark or Paul Clyro had been, with half of her face shot away, a dark-haired woman in a flowered trouser suit.

For a moment that seemed everlasting, Richard thought that it was Anne. He knew of no reason why Anne should be there, dead or alive, but the blue-black hair, the trouser suit, were surely hers.

It was a moment that taught him a great deal about himself, because in it he suffered an extremity of loss that he had never known it was in him to feel. There was actually a kind of relief in recognizing that he had made a fantastic mistake, relief which immediately began to seem an atrocious kind of callousness and which he wanted to forget as fast as he could.

The dead woman was Hazel Clyro. The dark hair was a wig. Her head was back against the cushions of the chair, with dried blood clotting the hair of the wig and staining the cushions. One of her hands hung over the arm of the chair, and just below it, on the floor, with her fingertips almost touching it, lay a revolver.

The eerie feeling that it had all happened before kept Richard rooted where he was. It was as if what was to happen next had been preordained. It would happen of itself. Nothing that he could do would affect it.

But that feeling passed and he advanced into the room.

A small suitcase stood on the floor near Hazel's chair and there was a milk-bottle beside it. In another chair were a light summer coat, a large shady hat and a red plastic handbag. Richard gave a light touch to the arm that hung down as if still reaching for the gun. *Rigor mortis* had come and gone and the arm was limp, moving faintly under his hand. He snatched it back, feeling that he was going to vomit. He could taste it in his mouth and feel the contraction of his stomach muscles.

But the spasm passed and he stood back, cold with shock, with moisture on his face. He began to look round for a telephone, as he had in the house in Vila do Bonfim. But here all you had to do was dial 999. That was easy. There was no language problem, no further need to take any action.

But before he dialled he suddenly thought of something that he wanted to do first. He thought of it as his glance fell on the red bag in the chair. He picked it up and looked inside for Hazel's passport.

It was there, a passport in the name of Margaret Chilmark, with Hazel's photograph in it. It was unmistakably Hazel's, although the woman of the photograph had dark hair. Richard gave a long sigh and returned the passport to the handbag. Some of the things that he had thought about during the long night began to fall into place. Inside the bag his hand encountered something else that roused his curiosity. It was a case of some sort, too large to be a spectacle case and not the right shape for a purse. He drew it out and opened it.

Inside there was a hypodermic syringe.

After that he looked through the rest of the contents of the bag and at the bottom, in a small phial without any label on it, he found the tablets. Very small, white tablets. He was fairly

137

sure what they were. He had once had a friend who had become addicted to heroin during a period of great pain after an operation, and the tablets that Richard had seen in his possession had looked just like these.

He wondered how long Hazel had been on drugs. How long had she carried the burden of that secret as well as all her others? What forlornness she must have lived through during the last three years, what loneliness and desperation, to explain it.

Of course, the drugs made a number of things clear. They and the passport, added together, began to build up a picture that made sense, simple sense, rather than a frenzied abstract that defied interpretation. He turned back to the telephone.

The doorbell rang.

It startled him violently. Then he realized that it was probably the milkman, who was trying to find out, in view of the bottles left on the doorstep, whether or not to leave any milk today. Richard decided not to answer the bell. He would wait here silently until he had heard the man's footsteps depart, then would make his call to the police.

But the footsteps did not depart and Richard realized that the man had probably just been having a chat with the woman from upstairs, and that she would have told him that Richard had gone round to the back of the house and had not re-emerged. Probably she was suspicious and scared. She might be out there on the doorstep now with the milkman, waiting to see what happened when he rang. The two of them might even have taken a look into the back yard and found the broken window. They might be whispering together about calling the police themselves. Richard decided that it would be best to answer the bell.

He went to the front door and opened it.

It was not the milkman who stood there. It was Jeannie Ottershaw.

She gasped, 'Richard!' and shot past him into the house.

She had on a raincoat and a silk scarf over her grey hair. She had no make-up on and her face was extremely pale. Richard noticed that there was no car in front of the house except his own. She had either come by taxi or had walked from the bus stop.

138

He closed the door and without saying anything let her go ahead of him into the sitting-room.

She took one pace into it, then stood stock still, pressing both fists to her mouth. Her eyes went wide and glazed.

'Oh God!' she said in a strangled voice that came out high and shrill instead of on its usual deep note. 'Oh God!'

But after that she seemed to gain control of herself. She dropped her hands, and though she went no farther into the room, her voice was more normal when she spoke again.

'Have you called the police, Richard?'

'I was just going to when you rang,' he answered.

'Well, go on and do it.'

But before he had reached the telephone, she said, 'Wait a minute. What are you doing here? Tell me. I don't understand it.'

'I got back from Madeira last night, as you know,' he said. 'I badly wanted to tell Hazel about what had happened there. I tried to telephone her several times and couldn't get an answer. I got worried, so I came round, and saw these curtains drawn and the light on inside.'

'How did you get in?' Jeannie asked. 'She hadn't given you a key, had she?'

'No, I never got as far with her as that.'

'How far *did* you get?' Her voice sharpened oddly.

'Not far at all. Not even as far as I thought. For instance, I didn't know about the heroin. Naïve of me, I can see now. The symptoms were all there. Her moodiness, her curious eyes, her caution with drink – that's characteristic of the addict, isn't it? – her indifference to her surroundings and the withdrawn kind of life she led. I suppose the stuff *is* heroin, isn't it? There's a phial of tablets in her bag.'

Jeannie gave a slight shudder, then her stiff body seemed to relax a little inside the loose raincoat.

'I'm afraid so. We tried to warn you, you know, Jerome and I, when we saw you'd got interested in her. We didn't want to come right out and say it, because we didn't know you well enough to feel we knew what you might think you had to do about it. We were working on her ourselves to take a cure. We were optimistic at first, but lately we'd begun to lose hope. We never knew where she got the stuff, though I think it was from

139

one of those unscrupulous doctors. We often used to feel there were all kinds of things about her we didn't know, although we were supposed to be friends. I used sometimes to feel afraid too that she had an urge to destroy herself – as she has.'

'Has she?' Richard said.

'What do you mean – has she?'

'Can you think of any woman who'd commit suicide, wearing a wig?' he asked.

Jeannie frowned. 'Yes, that's odd, isn't it? But you can see it's suicide.'

'I can't.'

'What do you mean?'

'I've only just begun to think it out. But there's what happened in Madeira.'

'You've been very mysterious about what happened in Madeira,' Jeannie said. 'Suppose you tell me about it.'

'Now? Or shall I call the police first?'

'Now,' she said abruptly.

'Then suppose we go into the other room,' he suggested. 'I don't like the idea of holding a sort of lecture across the poor girl's body.'

'In here will do,' Jeannie said. She even moved a little closer to the body, though she went on looking at Richard. 'Go on, what happened?'

'You're used to telling other people what to do, aren't you, Jeannie?' He moved across to a sofa near the fireplace and sat down. The back of the chair that held Hazel's body cut off most of his view of it. That helped a little. 'Well, to go right back to the beginning – '

'I know the beginning,' Jeannie said. 'It was when Hazel saw that film they made from the book, *Taken As Red*, and made up her mind Gavin Chilmark was Paul Clyro.'

'That wasn't anywhere near the beginning,' Richard replied. 'The beginning was years ago, when Hazel and Wolsingham fell in love with each other.'

'Hazel and *Wolsingham*?' she said incredulously.

'Yes. Hazel once told me she'd been in love with only one man in her life and of course I thought she meant Clyro – she meant me to think it was Clyro – but it was Wolsingham. They

140

fell in love up there at that place near Overscaig, when he was working for the Russians. And Paul Clyro hadn't a suspicion of anything – of the love-affair, or the spying either. But Wolsingham found out that the MI5 people had got on to him, and preparations were made for his flight. For his and Hazel's together. They were given passports in the names of Gavin and Margaret Chilmark, and Gavin was described as a journalist, and Margaret was to dye her hair black or wear a black wig to cover that very noticeable hair of hers, and they were to bolt, I suppose, along some prearranged escape route.'

'How do you know all this?' Jeannie asked. 'You talk as if you were quite certain of it.'

'I spent most of last night thinking,' Richard answered, 'and I've seen the Wolsingham passport, and there's some evidence here . . . Well, as you know, Wolsingham left things too late, so he killed himself. And Clyro found the body. He found the passport too. He must have, because he used it later. I suppose it was in Wolsingham's pocket, or a drawer of his desk. And I shouldn't be surprised if Clyro discovered he understood a lot of things then about how the Institute had been run that had puzzled him. But out of a sort of mistaken loyalty to the man he'd venerated, or perhaps simply to the Institute itself, hoping he could save it from a scandal, he concealed the passport and kept it concealed for a long time. What he didn't know then was that his wife had one to go with it. It's in that red bag over there.'

Jeannie pressed a hand to her mouth again, as if she were holding back something that she wanted to say, but after a moment of silence, she let the hand drop.

'Well, go on,' she said.

'You know what happened next,' Richard said. 'The Clyros weren't happy at Overscaig, so Jerome helped Paul Clyro get a job at that other place – '

'Blofield,' Jeannie said.

'Yes. And still they weren't happy. Paul believed everyone he met suspected him of having been in with Wolsingham, and Hazel was unhappy quite simply because her heart was broken.'

Jeannie shook her head. 'You didn't know Hazel very well, Richard. She'd never have got mixed up in spying. If there was ever a person who was completely indifferent to politics, it was Hazel. She'd no more have thought of working for the Communists than – than – ' She shrugged her shoulders, as if she could not think of a comparison.

'I know,' Richard said. 'She told me at our first meeting that politics didn't mean anything to her, and I believed her. I still do. But I think I know what happened. She was simply so indifferent that it didn't matter to her what the man she loved believed in. If anything, she'd a sort of contempt for beliefs and ideas of all kinds, because of the way they divide people. She'd suffered enough through that herself. Wolsingham himself was all that mattered to her.'

'But she stayed with Paul.'

'Oh yes. Why not? I expect she was still quite fond of him at that time.'

'But he left her. Why did he do that? Why did he wait for a year and then suddenly leave?'

'There's only one answer I can think of to that question. He found her passport.'

'The Chilmark passport?'

'Yes, and it told him that she'd meant to leave with Wolsingham. A second betrayal. So he decided to go. To clear out, leave all the old misery and dirtiness behind him. And as he already had a forged passport in his possession, and as he could make himself up to look sufficiently like the man in the photograph to get by, he decided to shed his old identity and start completely afresh.'

'But he took no money, no clothes, nothing. He simply walked out one morning and vanished into thin air.'

'Did he? He took a passport, we know that now. So he may have had clothes and money too that Hazel didn't know about. It was a planned disappearance, anyway. He wanted simply to vanish into that thin air and be forgotten.'

Jeannie nodded. 'You may be right. But the fact is, Richard, you still haven't said anything that isn't guesswork.'

'I'd say it was legitimate deduction from the evidence,' Richard answered. 'You see, I met Clyro. I talked to him. I talked to the girl he was living with. And I saw the Chilmark passport with the photograph of Wolsingham in it. I know it

142

was Wolsingham. I saw a press photograph of him yesterday. And also I talked at some length to the police in Madeira.'

'Madeira!' she said. 'At last we've got to Madeira. What *did* happen there?'

Richard's body tensed a little on the sofa. His eyes held Jeannie's eyes.

'As if you didn't know,' he said softly.

'I?' she said. Her forehead wrinkled. 'Have you some idea Hazel got in touch with me before – before she died? I hadn't heard anything of her for days – not since I saw you, when you told me you were going to Madeira.'

Richard shook his head. 'It wasn't Hazel who got in touch with you. It was Arthur Codsall.'

She looked puzzled. 'Who's he?'

'Arthur Codsall, of course, is the man you – they – used to keep an eye on Hazel once you realized she was on drugs and might be a hazard to you if she talked irresponsibly when the mood was on her. Because she knew all about you and Jerome from the Wolsingham days. Jerome was his link, wasn't he, with his foreign bosses? – Jerome who's always travelling all over the world, going to congresses, meeting scientists, and whose great asset is that air of bumbling innocence of his, which I believe is almost real. He'd never have got into the spying game if you hadn't pushed him into it. I wonder why you did it, Jeannie. You've got money and looks and position. What was missing? Was it just that you couldn't stand being married to a mere A E I O U? Because that's all Jerome would ever have been, left to himself. But a spy must have a wonderful sense of power. He's the one who knows what nobody else knows. He's the one who holds us all in the hollow of his hand. Power's so much more splendid than money, or comfort, or even happiness, isn't it?'

Jeannie gave him a long, thoughtful look, then said on a note of quiet astonishment, 'I believe you're mad.'

'A little, probably, just at the moment,' Richard said. 'Finding Hazel like this – is it surprising? I was in love with her, you know, I was quite a lot in love with her. But as I told you, I did a lot of thinking last night, so just for once I'll let myself go, shall I? I think you took me for an A E I O U too, and thought

143

I'd be quite easy to manage. Perhaps I am one. I'm never going to shine in this world. But that doesn't mean I have to be a complete fool. When you and Jerome tried so hard to discourage me seeing too much of Hazel, or at any rate taking too much notice of what she said by warning me about her mental state, it did just cross my mind that you might have some reason for this you weren't telling me. And then there was Codsall. He first came into my life the night I went to your party and took Hazel home afterwards. He followed us there, and let himself be seen. His job, of course, was to intimidate her, to remind her that if she ever talked out of turn, her life wouldn't be worth much. A secondary use he may have had is that when she saw him she was so frightened that she acted very peculiarly, and that may have put some people off wanting to get to know her better. But you know, Jeannie, it was a mistake to send him after me to Madeira. You should have kept him here to see that Hazel didn't go there herself. A live Gavin Chilmark in Vila do Bonfim was no danger to you. All he wanted was to be left in peace. But a dead Paul Clyro's going to be a fearsome danger. He'll be quite easily identified by his fingerprints, the police over there told me, and after that our police will soon come questioning you and Jerome.'

'Why me and Jerome?' She had not moved, but she was stiff again and her gaze held something new, the glitter of intense, frightened rage.

'Because of Codsall,' Richard answered.

'I tell you, I've never even heard of him before,' she said.

'Oh come. He was on the plane with me on Friday. He followed me about there, he picked me up and talked to me. He picked up the girl who was living with Clyro. He wanted to find out all he could about Clyro. But how did he ever find out I was going to Madeira except through you and Jerome? Besides my brother and sister-in-law, and Hazel herself, and Anne, you were the only people who knew I was going there. I didn't even tell my secretary where I was going. I felt self-conscious about it. I didn't spread it around. Yet Codsall went out on the same plane with me.'

'Chance,' Jeannie said, 'if he even matters, which I don't believe.'

Richard shook his head. 'The police won't think it's chance because of what I'll also tell them about Hazel's murder.'

'What is there to tell?' she asked defiantly.

'A good deal, when you put it all together. First about Wolsingham, the passports, Clyro's desertion. Then about what happened when I took her to the cinema. Of course it wasn't that title, *Taken As Red*, that made her nearly collapse. I rather doubt if she and Clyro had ever talked of writing a book together. Certainly the love scenes, which she claimed to recognize, were written by somebody else. But it was the name Gavin Chilmark that gave Clyro away and made her nearly faint there in her seat. Then she begged me to find out for her where he lived. I did it through Anne. Then I suggested going to Madeira myself, to find out if this man really was Clyro. I had some idea of getting things cleared up, persuading her to divorce him, perhaps getting her to marry me . . . ' His even voice went dry for a moment. 'Well – what was I saying? – Oh yes, I suggested going to Madeira and she wasn't specially keen on the idea, but I went ahead with it all the same. She didn't try to stop me. I don't think she cared whether I went or not, because she'd already made up her mind what she was going to do. She was simply going to go to Madeira herself to kill Clyro.'

'In God's name, why?' Jeannie exclaimed. 'Even if any of what you say is halfway true – about Hazel – about Wolsingham – not about Jerome and me – Clyro, as you said yourself, was no danger to her.'

'But she wanted revenge,' Richard answered. 'She'd been living for it for a long time. She thought it was Clyro who'd betrayed Wolsingham. She thought it because he'd got that passport. The irony is, of course, that Clyro can't have betrayed him. If he had, he'd certainly have left that passport to be found, he'd never have hidden it.'

She nodded. 'Yes, I see that.'

'It's a pity Hazel didn't. But the heroin explains a good deal, the clouded way she thought about the whole thing, and the fantastic confidence with which she carried out the murder. Think of it, she simply put that gun there in her handbag and sailed through customs with it, feeling sure she'd never be questioned. I suppose she'd got hold of the gun during the

Wolsingham days. And in Funchal she went to a hotel and got the manageress to ring up Gavin Chilmark for her, and arranged to meet him next morning. In the morning she took a taxi to his house, told the driver to wait, went in, shot Clyro, took the taxi to the airport and came home. The only precautions she took, I believe, were insisting on seeing Clyro quite alone, and wearing a dark wig, and using that false passport instead of her own. She must have imagined that a broad trail left by a non-existent woman called Margaret Chilmark was all the protection she needed. And she must have got home on Sunday night thinking that she'd been very successful. What she didn't realize was that it was just here that she needed protection – and hadn't got it.'

Jeannie spoke calmly. 'You understand, don't you, that everything you've said so far points to its being suicide. To have gone off like that to kill Clyro, yes, I can just manage to see her doing it. But as soon as she got home, she'd have gone to pieces. She wouldn't have been able to endure the thought of what she'd done. She'd have killed herself for certain.'

'Given time, I think she might have. Or she might have gone to the police and given herself up. But she wasn't given time to do that, and she didn't kill herself. Look around you, Jeannie. Do you mean you can see her arriving home, picking up the Sunday morning milk-bottle as she came in, then dumping it and her suitcase on the floor, plumping down in a chair and shooting herself – without taking off that wig? To me that's against nature. If she'd been going to kill herself, I'm sure she'd have taken off the wig. I think she'd have put the milk in the refrigerator, or at least taken it to the kitchen. I think she'd have taken her suitcase to her bedroom and perhaps even unpacked it. And I think, though I'm not sure, that she'd have written a letter for the police to find, explaining the execution she'd carried out on her husband. And also I think she'd then have lain down on her bed and done the job with a big overdose of heroin, rather than with the gun. No more violence, just wonderful oblivion. That's what I think would have happened.'

'But you can never count on people acting as you expect them to,' Jeannie said. 'You know that.'

'But I'm just coming to the proof.'

146

'Proof that she was murdered?'

'Yes, and by whom.'

'Somehow I doubt that,' Jeannie said. 'Try telling this story to the police and see if they've the same idea of proof as you have.'

'I will. But now shall I go on and tell you what happened when Hazel got home?'

'Yes,' she said. 'Go on.'

'She came in and she came face to face with someone who'd been in here, waiting for her. Someone who had a key to the flat and so could get in. Someone who'd been telephoned from Madeira by Arthur Codsall and told what had happened. He'd found Clyro dead just before I did. He'd gone in to see him, I suppose just to try and get friendly with him, because he must have known that Clyro's girl and I would be arriving in a few minutes, and we could all get chummy, and he might find out quite a lot. It looks as if he was trying to find out for you if the man was Clyro or not, and if he was, whether he could be any danger to you. But when he found Clyro dead, Codsall made off as fast as he could and put a call through to you and told you about the murder. So Jerome came here and waited. Waited, knowing about what time Hazel would get home if she'd really been to Madeira, and wondering if she'd really done the murder. Because, if she had, you couldn't allow her to live. If the police caught up with her, she'd soon break down and tell them everything, including all about the two of you. So Jerome came here . . . I've been assuming it was Jerome who came, not you, because I don't think you'd have made all the blunders he did. You'd have understood that point about the wig. If you'd had to kill her before she'd taken it off, you'd have taken it off afterwards and got rid of it somehow. And you'd have made this room look a bit more convincing. But Jerome isn't the type that makes an efficient criminal. He was waiting here for Hazel when she got home. He must have been waiting inside, because if she'd got here first and he'd rung the bell, she'd never have gone to answer the door in the wig. The very first thing she'd have done on getting home would have been to take it off. So he was waiting here and she came in and turned on the light and drew the curtains. And he saw her disguise and knew that it was as you'd feared, it was she who'd killed Clyro. So Jerome attacked her. How did he mean to kill her? Strangling? A blunt instrument? He can't have meant to shoot her, because it looks as if it's her own gun he used, and he couldn't have known that she'd be carrying it with her. She might have got rid of it somewhere on the journey. Anyhow, she just had time to get the gun out of her bag, but not to use it, when he got it away from her and used it on her. Then he dumped her in that chair, with the gun beside her, and fled.'

Jeannie was watching him thoughtfully. She now seemed to be taking an almost impersonal interest in the story. After a slight pause, she said, 'You still haven't supplied that proof you promised me.'

'Jerome had a key,' Richard said.

'Well?'

'I don't know how you got hold of it. Perhaps Hazel left one with you sometime or other when she went away. She never left one with any of her neighbours, but I think she might have with you. Or perhaps you got hold of a copy somehow, so that you could spy on her – and that key's in your handbag now, Jeannie. You didn't come here this morning on the off-chance of finding someone in. It was a big shock when you did find somebody. You only rang the bell as a precaution, in case the body had already been discovered and the police were here. If they were, you'd your story ready about being worried about Hazel. But you weren't really expecting anybody. You were going to let yourself in and put right all the things you'd found out from Jerome he'd done wrong. Lady Macbeth saying to her husband, "Give me the daggers . . . " You've got that key, Jeannie. And I'm coming for it.'

He stood up.

He added, 'If you haven't got it, I'll take back every single thing I've said.'

He took a step forward.

He knew that he was stronger than Jeannie and that there was no chance that she could escape through the door without his being able to stop her. He only had to move fast and get her handbag away from her.

She moved faster than he did. She stooped, straightened and faced him with Hazel's gun in her hand.

'I'll use this, Richard – don't think I won't,' she said. 'Stay where you are.'

Richard knew that there was no point in staying where he was. He would only be a stationary target instead of a moving one. He lunged at her, throwing himself sideways as he did so. He had a curious impression that someone was shouting. At the same time he felt a flash of pain beyond belief and as if at the same time a house had fallen on him and then there was nothingness. With blood coming bursting out of a hole in his chest, he lay on the floor only a few inches away from the dangling hand of Hazel Clyro.

Chapter Eleven

It was the milkman who saved Richard's life. It was the voice of the milkman, shouting, that he had heard the instant before he lost consciousness. The man had had a discussion of some length with the woman from upstairs. She had come down, still in her dressing-gown, with the pink plastic rollers in her hair, as soon as she heard the clink of milk-bottles in the street. She had told him about the stranger who had asked for Mrs Clyro, then disappeared round the house and not re-emerged. They had talked over the significance of this for some time, torn between curiosity, the desire not to become involved in something that struck them as just possibly dangerous, and the desire to do their duty, to act responsibly. This last, after much repetition of the arguments for and against each course of action, had finally won, and the milkman had gone cautiously along the path past the dustbins and coal bunker, and had found the broken window.

Seeing that, he had not given himself much time to think. If he had, he would no doubt have returned to the street and summoned a policeman. But he happened to be a man with a great sense of order, and also more bravery than he himself was aware of. The sight of the broken window, swinging open, offended his sense of order, while his bravery made it clear to him that something had to be done about it at once. Getting a knee up on the windowsill, as Richard had before him, he hauled himself up, climbed over the sink and had just jumped to the floor at the moment when Jeannie stooped for the gun.

Her voice, raised and excited, had given him some warning of what he was to find. He had charged into the sitting-room, shouting in horrified protest. Jeannie, taken completely by surprise, had let the gun in her hand waver, and the bullet had made a hole in Richard's shoulder instead of his heart.

She did not wait to correct this error. The sight of the stranger roaring at her from the doorway completely unnerved her. For all she knew, he had not come into the house alone. All she wanted was to get away. Turning the gun on him, she hissed at him to stand aside, which he hastily did, then she fled to the front door. Coming out, she came face to face on the doorstep with the woman from upstairs. The woman began to scream at the top of her voice, but also stepped swiftly out of Jeannie's way. Jeannie went running down the street and round the corner to where she had left the car. Getting into it she drove away, while the milkman, not feeling as brave as before, but guided by common sense, grabbed the telephone and still shouting from sheer shock, yelled for the police and an ambulance.

Richard floated back to consciousness late that afternoon. He had been operated on and heavily dosed with a pain-killing drug. The drug had an odd effect upon him. It filled him with an airy sense of self-confidence, made him feel that there was almost nothing that he did not understand, that the mystery of the universe, of life and death, was a mere nothing.

The feeling was not as pleasant as might be supposed. It was distinctly frightening to be burdened with so much knowledge, and so unlike his normal way of feeling that he felt he might easily commit some foolishness concerning it.

He did not take in much about his surroundings. He was in a long, rather shabby ward of one of London's older hospitals. There were two rows of neat beds, in some of which the occupants were bandaged and inert, in some recovering and restless, and in one or two had the purple, pulpy faces with which they had been rescued from road-accidents or street brawls. Somewhere in the middle of the ward a television was chattering away, as essential, probably, to the cure of some of the patients as it was detrimental to that of the others. Richard hardly noticed it. He had just decided that it was essential for him to attract the attention of one of the nurses and explain to her immediately some enlightenment that he had just been given about the late massacre of Glencoe.

Why the massacre of Glencoe should have been on his mind at just that time he was never to know, and at the moment it did not occur to him to wonder. He simply knew that it was of the greatest importance to communicate to someone now, instantly, while it was still so clear in his mind, his insight into what had happened in that grey rocky place in the northern mountains.

A place not so very far from Overscaig . . .

Was that the reason, he wondered later, why the massacre had occupied his lost thoughts while the surgeon probed and stitched and bandaged? At least, Glencoe and Overscaig were both in the north-west of Scotland, a region in which he had intended to spend his holiday before he had changed his plans and gone to Madeira. Perhaps the two thoughts had jostled one another and become all mixed up.

Meanwhile, however, it was urgent to explain to some intelligent and responsive person that the important thing about the massacre had not been the number killed. That, as massacres went, was practically minimal. But the reason why it had achieved its infamous place in history was simply that it was a classic example of the betrayal of trust. Men had been given hospitality in good faith, then had turned on and slaughtered their hosts. Trust, he wanted to explain to somebody, has its own laws. These are not necessarily the same as those of the state. They may ignore beliefs and customs. They may override contracts. But they place the highest of all demands on the individual. It is an abomination to betray trust . . .

The little nurse whose attention he succeeded in attracting agreed with everything he said. She answered, 'Yes, dear, I think so too.' But perhaps she was not as intelligent and responsive as she seemed, for she immediately hurried away and

151

brought to his bedside a severe-looking Sister, who felt his pulse, frowned faintly when he tried to talk to her, obviously did not listen to what he had to say, then went away again.

The little nurse then brought him another visitor, an unusually tall, burly man who sat down at Richard's bedside and took a notebook out of his pocket. The nurse drew the curtains round the bed and said, 'Only a minute or two, mind. Probably you won't find he knows what he's talking about,' which irritated Richard, because he had never felt so clearly that he knew exactly what he was talking about. Luckily the big man seemed to understand this, for after a moment he put the notebook away and listened with interest to what Richard had to tell him.

Then all of a sudden he was not there any more. The man, the chair, the curtains that cut Richard off from the long ward, had all vanished, and when he became conscious again he was not sure that any of it had happened.

The routine of hospital life began, the early wakening, the dressings, the drugs, the thermometer. The walls of the ward were painted a pale green, gone dingy from the London atmosphere, and on the ceiling above Richard's bed there was an intricate pattern of cracks in the plaster, into which he felt a compulsion to read some meaning. He could see a face in it, but also it was obviously a map of some unknown country. Every face, he thought deeply, is the map of an unknown country, only some just a little more unknown and undiscovered than others. When the big man reappeared, proving that he had not been a mere drug-induced delusion, Richard tried to explain this to him, but once the thought had been put into words it did not seem very important any more.

The big man, who, he was told, was a Superintendent, put quiet questions to him. This was difficult for Richard, because although he knew that most of the answers must be lodged somewhere in his memory, he could not remember many of them. There was a darkness in his mind that obscured not merely the shot that Jeannie had fired and its impact with his flesh and bone, but also some minutes before it. So he had to work out his argument again, step by step.

'I'm sorry, it's that stuff they give me,' he apologized when he felt that he had been more than usually dense. 'They told me the name of it, but I forget it. It's a morphia derivative, not as addictive as heroin . . . Oh yes, heroin . . . You were asking me something about heroin, weren't you? Had I any suspicion she was using it? . . . No, I'd no suspicions of anything to speak of. I saw her face, I saw all their faces, and never suspected anything. I didn't see they were maps as well and that I ought to be able to read them . . . Oh, there I go again, talking nonsense. You'll have to bear with me. But tell me, Superintendent, don't you think there's only spying because some people are naturally spies? It's a talent they've got, and it's because they need an outlet for their talent that we have all this nonsense. I mean, everyone finds out everything about everyone else sooner or later, and trying to stop them doing it must be fearfully expensive, but even if spying was internationalized and put under the control of the United Nations, we'd still have spies nosing out some new angle on things, and working away as hard as ever, because there are people who have this strange need to betray trust. It's the way they're made. They can't help it. I suppose there's a lot of hatred and envy at the back of it . . . I'm sorry, I'm talking too much. It's that stuff. You did say you'd arrested the Ottershaws, didn't you?'

'They aren't under arrest,' the Superintendent answered. 'We apprehended them at Heathrow, just in time to stop them leaving for Stockholm, which was not, I imagine, meant to be the end of their journey, and at the moment they're helping us with our inquiries. So is a man called Arthur Codsall, a private detective with a habit of sticking a thumb into some very nasty pies. Now about that evening when you returned from Madeira, Mr Hedon, and tried to telephone Mrs Clyro . . .'

Step by step he took Richard over the events of that evening and the following morning, until the story of them had become clear in his mind again, with most of the gaps filled in.

He had other visitors besides the police. The first whom he remembered clearly was his sister-in-law, Harriet, though she told him that both Bernard and Anne had come to see him before and had reported that he had spoken to them lucidly.

Dimly he remembered that they had come. He had an impression that with Anne he had not spoken at all, but had only clutched her hand, afraid that perhaps she was not there at all and would slip away into the shadows if he let her go for an instant. For he had had one frighteningly convincing delusion. It had been during his first night in the hospital, and it had been so convincing that it had taken him a day or two to assure himself that it could not have happened.

He had thought that Hazel Clyro had come into the ward and had sat down by his bed and taken a notebook out of her big red plastic handbag and begun to ask him questions. They were all nonsensical questions. He had no memory of them. But he remembered her manner, aloof and stern and reproving, as if he had failed her somehow and she had come back to make sure that he did not forget it. Then she was gone, leaving him with his knowledge of that failure. For might he not have helped her if he had taken more trouble to read the maps in faces, instead of simply play at being in love with her? That had been the easy thing to do, but not the wise, the helpful.

Not that there had ever been much chance of helping her. The power to love had dried up in her with the death of Wolsingham, and only hatred and revenge and the need for oblivion had remained. Perhaps Jerome Ottershaw had not done her a bad turn by helping her to the oblivion with a mercifully swift hand.

Harriet brought him a jar of home-made greengage jam.

'Are you eating properly?' she asked. 'Is the food all right? Are the nurses nice, or do they keep you waiting ages when you want a bedpan? The only time I was in hospital – that was when I had my gall bladder trouble d'you remember? – I had the fight of my life over bedpans. I had to get hold of the Sister, I said to her, "Sister, I have never in my life made an unnecessary fuss over anything, and I have no patience with the kind of people who do. So kindly understand that when I holler for a bedpan, it means I need a bedpan." She took it very badly. She took it as a personal criticism. She was the kind of woman you can't talk to reasonably. We never got along. My experience of nurses is that they're either angels from heaven or sadistic bitches. The power they have over you brings out one or the other quality in them. Which are yours?'

'On the angelic side, if anything,' Richard answered. 'I've

154

no complaints. The food has a sort of all-over grey look, but I'm not much interested in the subject, anyway.'

'Well, we'll soon feed you up again when we get you home,' Harriet said. 'And another time, pay a little more attention when I warn you about people. I was right about those friends of yours, wasn't I?'

'Harriet, dear, you're almost always right,' Richard said, 'which is all but insufferable. I don't know how Bernard stands it.'

She laughed and gave a friendly pat to the hummock in the bedclothes made by his feet.

'He nearly always agrees with me,' she said. 'We hardly ever argue. He's much more sensible than you.'

'I've always known that.'

'You know, we've both been terribly upset about you. To get yourself mixed up in a thing like this and actually *shot* . . . It isn't the sort of thing that happens to people like us.'

'I'll do my best to see that it doesn't happen again.'

'Yes, mind you do.' She got up, bent over him and kissed him. 'I hope you like the jam. I made it while you were in Madeira. It's turned out very well. I'm leaving the choice of some reading-matter for you to Bernard. He'll be in to see you this evening.'

She departed, having brought as her most important gift something that she had not mentioned, a sense of normality. The atmosphere of fantasy in which Richard felt that he had been enshrouded for days began to clear. He began to feel more like himself again. What had happened had happened, there was no cure for it, but life would go on.

Bernard came to see him that evening. But before he came, Richard had another visitor. She took him by surprise, coming slowly along the ward towards his bed, looking with open curiosity at the occupants of all the others, and distributing encouraging smiles to right and left. Gillian Acheson was in a shiny black plastic raincoat, with black plastic boots up to her knees, and had her fair hair swept up almost out of sight under a black plastic rainhat, perched rakishly high on her head. On seeing her, Richard wondered for a moment if this could be her idea of mourning, then decided that it was more probable that the thought had not occurred to her. She was carrying something done up in pale blue tissue paper.

'Hallo,' she said gravely.

'Hallo, Gillian,' Richard replied.

'Do you mind my coming to see you?' she asked. 'I mean, if I'm too much for you, just send me away. I'll understand.'

'I couldn't be more delighted to see anyone,' he said.

'Just as long as you mean that.' She put her package down on his knees. 'I hope you'll like them.'

'Could you open it for me?' he said. 'I've only one usable hand.'

'Of course. How stupid of me.' She stripped away the wrapping paper and revealed an enormous bunch of red roses. 'I got them cheap,' she said. 'I've just started working in a flower shop. I don't suppose they'll last very long, they aren't this morning's, but at least they'll be nice for a day or two.'

'They look wonderful and luxurious,' Richard said. 'Sit down.' When she had, he went on, 'So they let you leave Madeira.'

'Yes, they seemed quite glad to see the last of me, actually.'

'Where are you living now?'

'With the aunts in Twickenham. It's funny, now that I've been away from them, I realize how very sweet they are. They've been so good to me in their funny fashion, much more upset at my having lost poor Gavin than they were at my taking up with him. I don't think they're really able to get properly angry with anybody, that's why they do such funny things. They just don't know about anger. They don't believe anyone could ever get angry with them, when they mean so awfully well. And almost nobody does. Of course, I can't stay with them. I should be as nutty as they are in no time. And an alcoholic too. The number of sherry bottles those two old dears smuggle out to the dustbin when they think I'm not looking! D'you know, their neighbour, Mr Evesham, buys the stuff for them, because they don't think it would be ladylike to go into the pub at the corner, which keeps very good sherry, and buy it themselves. They don't even like ordering it from the grocer by telephone. But they trust Mr Evesham not to give away their little secret, so he does their shopping and hands the bottles over the back garden fence where no one can see.'

'And has Mr Evesham kept their secret?' Richard asked.

'Of course not. Honestly, how could anyone be expected to keep a thing like that to himself? Everyone in the street knows all about it. But they're nice enough not to let on that they do. But, Richard – here am I, talking away like this and I haven't even asked you how you are. How *are* you? I must say, you look terrible.'

'I feel it.'

Her face became tender with concern. It was very beautiful when it looked like that. It had not yet lost its deep, healthy tan, but there was a faint haggardness about it that added several years to her apparent age.

'It's dreadful – everything that's happened, isn't it? I do hope you get well soon. When I think of how happy I was . . . Was it wrong to be so happy, d'you think? I mean, when one had never done anything much to deserve it. Was it tempting Providence? Not that I don't think that's a silly sort of thing to think. I think it's mostly a superstitious fear of letting oneself ever be so happy again, because now I know what it's like to lose it. I was just incredibly lucky, that's all, to have it at least once in my life. And I'll tell you one thing I've decided about the future. I'm going to stick to complete continence. But complete! Don't you think that's sensible? Because as I feel at present, you know, I could easily go in the opposite direction and become completely promiscuous. There's something fearfully tempting about it.'

'I expect you've chosen the better alternative,' Richard said, hoping, nevertheless, that a different one would appear before too long, and thinking that in spite of the present intensity of her sorrow, it probably would. 'How did you find me here, Gillian?'

'Don't you remember giving me your address and telephone number?' she said. 'When I got back to Twickenham I rang you up. But I couldn't get any answer, whatever time I rang, so I checked it in the book, in case I was ringing a wrong number, and I found your brother's number at the same address as yours, so I rang his, and your sister-in-law answered and told me what had happened and where you were. So I found out about visiting hours and came as soon as I could. When you're better, Richard, can I see you again and get your advice about some things?'

'Such as? I'm not sure I'm very good at giving advice.'

'Oh, jobs, places to live, making some sense of my life. I won't be a nuisance, I promise, but if I could just talk . . . No, as a matter of fact, I'm trying to screw up my courage to ask you if you'd think of giving me a job in that bookshop of yours, something very, very lowly, like tying up parcels, but where I could start picking up some knowledge. The flower shop's fine for the moment, but I don't think it'll seem very interesting for long. I want something to get my teeth into and with a bit of a future. And I'm not all that illiterate, actually, and I pick things up fast, and I'm good at selling things. But I won't bother you with that now. Only if you'd just give it an occasional thought . . .'

'I'll do that,' Richard promised, reflecting that it would take more than an occasional thought to work out how to break it to Bernard that someone like Gillian might be coming to work in Farcet Street. It just might work out, however, if she honestly wanted it to, and Richard knew that he would like to help her, even if there was some danger of her trying to turn him into a father-figure in the process He would have to consider that angle rather carefully.

She chatted for a little longer, and left only a minute or two before Bernard appeared, bringing books and magazines for Richard.

Anne came next day. She and Harriet and Bernard had worked out a rota, so that they should not all arrive together. She had brought no presents with her, and sat down on the chair by his bed and fell into a silence. It did not feel strange. They were often silent when they were alone with one another. But there was something strange about her expression as she looked at him. Its faintly clownish mournfulness, at odds, as always, with her sharply crooked smile, seemed to be covering some unusual emotion, and doing so only with difficulty. Suddenly she laughed, and Richard realized that the emotion was mirth.

'What's funny?' he asked.

'You're looking far better,' she said. 'You'll be home in a few days.'

'Is that amusing?'

158

'It's splendid,' she answered. 'But there's the question of what our relationship will be then.'

'Our relationship . . . ?' A memory that had been hovering cloudily at the edges of Richard's consciousness for the last day or two took on a momentary clarity of outline. 'Anne, *did* I . . . ?'

'Richard, you did. That first evening, when I came to see you, you clung to my hand and said you loved me and had never loved anyone but me. You even asked me to marry you. But of course you were under the influence of drugs, and if it's off, I shan't sue. We'll go out and drink champagne on it, whichever way you want it.'

He let his head, which had come up with a start, drop back on the pillow. He lay remarkably still, his gaze on the cracks in the ceiling which made both a face and a map. The face perhaps he would forget with time, but the map surely never . . .

'The important question would seem to be,' he said, 'how did you answer – because you weren't under the influence of drugs.'

'Oh, I answered yes,' she said, 'as I ought to have long ago, even if you wouldn't get round to asking the right question. You were always afraid of Peter between us, weren't you?'

'Yes.' He brought his gaze down from the face on the ceiling and looked into hers.

'And I thought you were afraid of taking on an ageing widow with two children.'

'So Harriet was right. That's what she always said to me. And how happy it'll make her to be able to say so. Anne, my darling, what an awful lot of time we've wasted.'

'It might have been more if I hadn't had an awful nightmare that I was going to lose you.'

He was puzzled. 'But what did they tell you? This thing – ' he pointed to the wad of dressing on his shoulder, ' – it was never dangerous.'

'I didn't mean that. I meant, lose you to Hazel. Jealousy can be very instructive.'

'Jealousy? You? But you did nothing about it, never said anything, never showed anything . . . '

'No, I'm not very bright at understanding myself. But luckily you said the right things the other evening when I put the words into your mouth. Because that's what I did, you know. I took advantage of your state to put words in your mouth. I couldn't resist doing it. Suddenly it was so easy – and so very important.'

'I'm sure you couldn't have made me say a single thing I didn't want to. Of course, that drug they were giving me gave me an insane sort of confidence. I felt I knew everything, understood everything, could achieve anything . . . By the way, how are the children going to take this?'

'Oh, they approve. They say it's quite time they acquired a father.'

'So you told them . . . !'

She laughed and bent and kissed him.

The man in the next bed smacked his lips loudly. He had been brought into the ward on the same day as Richard, suffering from multiple injuries, as the result of having been pushed downstairs by his wife. She had come to visit the man every day since then, bringing him fruit, and cigarettes and once smuggling in a half-bottle of whisky, with which he had been very hospitable to the other patients in the ward. They were a devoted couple, who had achieved their own kind of strange stability in marriage.

'The visitors you get!' the man said. 'That nice little dolly girl with the roses, and now this, and all those coppers too, making you the centre of interest to all us insignificant blokes. I wonder what it is about you. Me, all I get is my old woman with grapes and apologies.'